Three Retired Detectives In Paradise

CD Grimes, Nick Storie, and Clint Faraday were in two books together. In the first they solved a murder in Bocas de Toro. In the last they move to an island on the comarca.

About the Author

CD began writing fiction in 1984 and has more than 300 books published as of 3/15/16 in SciFi, murder, orchid culture and various other fields.

He now resides Gualaca, Chiriqui, Panamá, where he continues research into epiphytic plants and plays music with friends. He loves the culture of the indigenous people and counts a majority of his closer friends among that group. He funds those he can afford through the universities where they have all excelled. "The Indios are very intelligent people, they are simply too poor (in material things and money.) to pursue higher education."

CD loves Panamá and the people, despite horrendous experiences (Free e-book; *Fading Paradise*). He plans to spend the rest of his life in the paradise that is Panamá

CD is involved in research of natural cancer cure at this time. It has proven effective in all cases, so far. It is based on a plant that has been in use for thousands of years, is safe, available, and cheap. He was cured of a serious lymphoma with use of the plant, *Ambrosia peruviana*.

Information about this cure is free on the FaceBook page Ambrosia peruviana for cancer. CD asks only that all who try it please report on its effectiveness on that group.

Three detectives originally from Florida meet in David, Panamá. Clint Faraday is retired from the US and is living on the Comarca Ngobe Bugle with his wife and son and daughter.

CD Grimes is a billionaire private detective from Bonita Springs, Florida. He is with his wife and flew in his own jet to David at the invitation of his nutty musician, botanist, author friend, Dave, who works with Clint Faraday quite often and is also a close friend of the Indios.

Nick Storie is there with his wife just to see the country. He has a place on Martinique. He is a police homicide detective with Naples South Station.

(Theses are the three detective series I wrote and am writing)

Dave finds a murder case for them. They can try to solve it, each with his own method.

It seems to be an ordinary sort of thing.

At first.

Contents

Clint Faraday, retired private detective from Florida, now residing on the Comarca Ngobe Bugle in Panamá, stretched and yawned. He went out on his porch overlooking the Caribbean in Cusapín with his first cup of coffee for the day. He was as much as addicted to the rich fine Panamanian coffee. It was really fresh, having been ground from the dried coffee beans his wife had brought from their hideaway place in the mountains near Quebrada Tula just yesterday afternoon.

It would be a good day. Beautiful sunrise.

Nito, his son, came with his daughter, Nicole, to hug him and head for the school in Cusapín. Clint and two friends had built several schools on the comarca, as well as hospitals and clinics.

His beautiful young (Clint was 69. Tyna was 28.) wife came to tease and play. She was going into Cusapín to help clean and sort the yuca, yampi, otoe and other root crop vegetables for storage and to take into Chiriqui Grande for the market.

"What are you doing today, Hon?" she asked, then thought. "Oh, yeah. Dave wants you to go to David to meet a friend from Florida he thinks you might know from being a detective there."

"I can handle the foundation and that kind of crap while I'm there. I'm getting a mite too old and cranky to have to go to David every time somebody sneezes.

"Dave wanted you to come."

"No. I'm sick of cities. I like it here."

"He said that he wanted to see the two most beautiful women in the world there together to watch the riots it would cause. Selma is going to be there. She knows the detective and his wife."

Selma Wentworth was Dave's ladyfriend. They had known each other in Florida before Dave moved to Panamá. She came to visit several years ago and, like Dave, never looked back at the states.

Like Clint, for that matter!

"You can run over to Soloy while you're there. I think the museum branch there is about the most popular place near David. The government is still trying every trick it can think of to get it moved to Panamá City."

A case Clint had led to the discovery of a preserved pirate ship that had what turned out to be eleven billion dollars worth of gold and jewels. (Book 51 :*Dead Man Talking*) Clint had arranged to have the entire find registered as property of the Ngobe, which was merely the law in the constitution. He got the official declaration before the government knew what it was worth. He had found pirate treasure before that was sent to Panamá City – where more than eighty five percent of it disappeared.

"Not going to happen. All the publicity from all over the world guarantees they can only go so far."

"Well, I guess you won't be here for a few days, so I can move my fantastic lover in while you're gone. The trouble with that is I can't find anyone who can even offer you a little competition!"

They teased a few minutes longer, then Tyna headed for the town a little more than a kilometer away along the beach. Clint packed enough for four days and got in his boat to head for Chiriqui Grande, from where he drove his own car to David.

The trip was beautiful, across the mountains and the dam. He stopped in Hornitos and Gualaca to visit with friends for a few minutes. He arrived in David and checked into the Pensión Costa Rica and went to the restaurant across the street in the panaderia, then called Dave, who said he was just heading for the airport to meet CD.

Clint said he brought the car, so he could take him and bring his friends into David. It would save them taxi fare, at least.

"He flies his own twelve seater Lear jet? He's worried about a three dollar taxi bill?"

The only detective Clint ever heard of in Florida who could own a two million dollar jet that he flew himself was CD Grimes. He'd met him in Sarasota on a case some years ago. It involved massive theft from NASA, thus the taxpayer. He knew what Dave meant about the two most beautiful women in the world. Alma Grimes was a total knockout.

"He'll want to go to the classy Hotel Ciudad David, I suppose."

"No. They'll stay at my Abanicos place. They aren't like you probably expect. CD talks a lot like he's a pompous ass, but it's his method. They're very real, very basic people."

"Well, I think we'll have a lot to talk about if he talks about his cases."

"Not too much. He likes fishing and seeing the country. He grows orchids, which is where I originally met him. Alma is as much into them. They'll be in heaven here!

"I send him a lot of the new things I find. We've already agreed to spend most of his time here all over the country."

"Hell's fire, Dave! You've been here twenty years and haven't seen half of it yourself! How long are they staying?"

"The nice thing about being a billionaire is that you stay as long as you damned well please!"

"It should prove interesting, at the very least!"

"Are you about ready?" Alma Grimes, wife of the semi-famous CD Grimes, billionaire private detective, called from the house. CD was in the cool house, a special greenhouse he had built underground so temperature and humidity could be controlled exactly.

"Just checking the autos," he replied. "Just think, love! We're going to the places Dave gathered a hundred or more of these plants. If Panamá is half of what the pictures tell, it's going to be a great vacation!"

"They're actual pictures. Dave doesn't change anything, so it will be just like that. I want to see the places he uses on the covers of his books."

"I think we'll really like Panamá. If that vacation place on Isla San Cristobál, his Indio friend's finca, is still available, I'll probably buy it."

"Well, we can certainly make an orchid garden there with native species! There are more than twelve hundred listed species and Dave has listed probably ten dozen more. Most of the places he'll show us were never explored before he did it."

"He'll show us a lot of places that have never been explored, so we can find a few new things for ourselves, knowing him. I can name one after you and you can name one after me!"

They joked a bit, ate a breakfast that was made from local seafoods they'd caught themselves, then got in the old Jeep CD liked and headed for the private airport in Englewood. Mike and Shirley talked awhile and they promised to say hello to Dave for them and to have them go to Panamá if it was half of what they expected.

Tony Jacobi, CD's manager for "The Crane Crap" – a bunch of companies CD owned, and husband of Shirley, came to see that things would run smoothly while they were gone.

"Hell, Tony. You run them anyhow. Get JK to take care of anything we normal people can't handle!"

JK was John Kiley. He was an absolute genius with computers. CD had never found a problem he couldn't fix.

After half an hour or so they got in the jet and headed for Panamá.

The flight over the gulf and Caribbean was smooth. CD took a short detour to fly over Kylvania, a group of islands southeast of Panamá that he had bought in a case and had given to JK. It was registered as an independent nation. He also flew over St. Wartons Island on the way, where he owned some property, as did Dave.

He landed at David and went through customs. He expected more trouble than he got. Dave was there with a person he wanted CD and Alma to meet who had a lot of pull with the police and local government, so they were passed through quickly.

From the Caribbean coast to David, which is near the Pacific, showed lush green jungles and few settlements. Volcan Barú is near, and was quite imposing. Dave had collected a lot of plants on the volcano and in the mountains between Chiriqui Grande, on the Caribbean, and David. He flew over the road to see the dam, which was a major spot where Dave had explored the first few years he was in the country. There were peaks as high as eighteen hundred meters.

Alma said she was sure she was going to like Panamá! It was truly beautiful, and they hadn't seen one city! Chiriqui Grande was a little fishing village!

They could see David wasn't like large cities, though it was second largest in Panamá. It was spread out.

There were a few fairly tall buildings, but not a clutter of ugly highrises or any of that. Dave had said, often, that it was a great big puebla. It has casinos and fine restaurants and malls and other trappings, but managed to stay more of a town.

The people they met, with one exception, were very friendly and curious. Alma was the center of attention as soon as she got off the jet, as always. She was a spectacular woman.

Dave was waiting with a well-built man CD would estimate to be fifty five to sixty years old. He looked a bit familiar. He was introduced as Clint Faraday.

"I've seen you somewhere before?" CD asked.

"Sarasota. Nineteen eighty eight. That NASA deal. Warne."

"That's twenty four years, so I'm a bit vague. You worked for the man in, where was it? Toward the center of the state and south?"

"I was checking up on the ex-wife, who turned out to be the biggest of the crooks. You used my testimony in her trial."

"But you were about forty five years old then! You can't be much over that now!"

"I'm sixty nine. Life is good here and you don't age so fast.

"I can see what Dave meant when he said he wanted my wife to come. There would be the two most beautiful women in the world! He was right!"

"How sweet!" Alma cried. "That Indian girl Dave sent pictures of? She can't be ... oh, yes. He said you married her and that you have two children."

"She's twenty four. I'm declared a Ngobe and she's Ngobe."

"I can picture you, Tyna, and Shirley Jacobi here. The world would never be the same!" Dave said. "Selma's got your rooms ready.

"I figure we can go to La Fortuna tomorrow and to the comarca in three days. We can stop in Cusapín for the night so you can meet Tyna and the kids. We can look over my collection there, then head to the wilds. I figured you'd rather go to places no one's ever been who knew the difference between and oak tree and an orchid."

"Didn't I tell you?" Alma said to CD, who grinned and nodded.

"Those boys are Indios," Alma said. "You said they're handsome. You're right."

"These are in the city too much. They're not like the comarca and mountain Indios. Those are gods next to these," Dave replied.

"Are these gay?" Alma asked. "They seem to spend a lot of time hugging each other!"

Clint laughed. "I don't think they're gay. We Ngobe touch a lot. I hug them and they hug me. It doesn't go much beyond that – with me. I understand Dave takes it further sometimes."

"Oh, yeah! That's another difference in here and the states," Dave said. "We look at things from a different cultural perspective. I'm among them most of the time and live in their culture, which beats ours hands-down!

"Let's get to the house. You'll be tired from the flight.

"How's JK? Still running the whole world with his comps?"

"We all wish he could, but that's gotten awfully complicated," CD answered. They talked about politics and such as they loaded the car and headed for Dave's rented house not very far from the airport.

Alma was as beautiful a woman as Tyna. She was also a normal woman, like Tyna. A couple of times Alma said, "CD!" when he started to give orders. Dave said he was used to running those huge corporations and had fifty people around ready to jump when he wanted anything. Alma was trying to break him of the habit. Just tell him to fuck off if he gave you any orders. Other than that, he seemed like a very good person.

"CD's used to having people jump because he's got so much money. He mostly ignores them, but it can get you into a bad habit," Alma said. "It's also his method with the detective thing. He goes into a case knowing that he *will* solve it. He can seem to be overbearing at times, but it works.

"My God! I don't think I want to drive here!"

Several taxis and two SUVs were jockeying for position. It looked like there would be a five car pile-up, but they managed to avoid actually hitting each other.

"Hah! This is nothing! Panamá City is an open demolition derby!" Dave said. "I always say the taxi drivers have to get a certificate from asshole school to hold a license here, but that's true of taxi drivers the world over.

"We can rest awhile, then I'll treat you to a meal at La Tipica. I know you like shrimp, and theirs is the best!"

"I'm paying for the food. No argument!" CD said.

"In the states, their shrimp plate would cost on the order of thirty five dollars a plate. Here, it's eight fifty," Clint said. "I'll pick you up at six?"

They agreed, but CD said they would take taxis. He heard they weren't so expensive here, either.

"From my place? Stand by the bus stop and you get a ride for sixty cents apiece to downtown. The Pedregal bus is thirty five cents. You can walk from my place to Las Brasas, which would be my second choice. Unbelievable ribeye steak! Same price. It would cost sixty bucks in the states!"

"The bus is only thirty five cents? What? Three blocks? Where is Pedregal?" Alma asked.

"Pedregal is across from the airport. Downtown is about five kilometers, I think. The marina at Pedregal is as far as the bus goes. Maybe seven kilometers. The bus is thirty five cents if you want to go one block or the whole distance," Dave explained. "Taxis are generally a dollar and a quarter to a dollar and a half. They take people to Pedregal and would return empty except for carrying passengers for sixty cents apiece. They generally carry five, so that's three dollars, the same as the trip from downtown to Pedregal. Panamá has a very good transportation system and the best roads in Central America."

"I can say that everything you've said about this places is exactly as you said it is," Alma said happily. "I already love the places and haven't been anywhere except at an airport and riding in a car!"

"It gets to you fast," Dave said. "I'll tell you about my first trip here someday!"

"You already did," she replied with an impish grin. "Like fifty times!"

"Here we are. See you at sixish," Clint said.

CD looked at the house and said, "This is what you pay three hundred a month for?"

"Uh-huh."

"In Florida it would be fifteen hundred plus maintenance plus electric, plus anything else."

"I do pay electric."

"How much?"

"Twenty one twelve last month. The few days we need the air conditioning it goes higher. One month it was thirty two whole dollars!"

"Sheesh!"

They went inside, where Selma greeted them. She and Alma got into a discussion of the changes in Florida and Panamá over the past few years since Selma moved there.

"You live here with Dave. I like this place!

"I suppose he spends most of his time in the jungles."

"I spend some time here, even when Dave's gone. I have my own place near Las Tablas. You'll love that place, too."

They talked a lot about the people. Alma said there seemed to be as many fat people there as the states anymore. Selma explained that a lot of the men liked bigger women. Out of the city there weren't so many.

They spent the next two days just roaming through the mountain forests, researching orchids.

"Oh, Nick! I was thinking I would hate this place from what we went through in Panamá City! This is really different and really nice, isn't it?" Janet Storie said to Nick as they went to get a taxi from Malek Airport in David, Panamá. "We flew over miles and miles of pure jungle! I thought it would be hot. Everyone said David is hot, but this is comfortable! Naples is easily ten degrees hotter, and without a breeze! It's exactly what Dave said in his e-mails.

"I wish we could have gotten in touch with him before we came. I'd like to see him. He's about eighty now, so probably doesn't get around like he used to.

"I have the phone number he sent four or five years ago, but he's probably moved by now. I would have to know the area code."

Nick laughed. Janet was excited. "I think the whole country is one area code, so all you'd have to do is dial the number. I'm sure it's changed by now, but you could try. What can it cost? A quarter?

They went out the door to the airport to flag a taxi. One came up and they put their bags in and got in. They said, "Where is a good medium-priced hotel?" He said the Best Western. Rooms from about fifty dollars. The taxi was six dollars.

"Oh! We know a man here! He told us about David! He says he knows a lot of people. They call him Dave. He has very white hair and..." Janet began.

"He runs around with Clint Faraday? That Dave? Plays the guitar and writes books?"

"Yes, that would be Dave!"

"I'll take you to the Alcalá. Nice, and thirty bucks double. Taxi's two bucks. Dave's a friend. He's done favors for my family. Clint, too."

"Do you know where we can find him?"

"He might be here or he might be out in the jungle somewhere. Mostly, it's in the jungle."

"I have a phone number, but it's five years old or more, so I don't suppose he has it anymore."

"He has it. He has a cheap cell he bought when he first came here and it still works. He had several expensive ones in between that don't work."

"Oh! I'll call him then! You say it's a cell phone?"

"Most of them are anymore. Lots of Blackberry and lots of those computer types. His is an old one. You can use mine."

He handed her his cellular."

"How kind! Thank you!" She punched the number and the call button. Nothing happened. She asked what she'd done wrong.

"You say the number was more than eight years ago?"

"Yes."

"Add a six in front. They changed to where all cell numbers begin with six."

She tried that. It rang three times, then Dave answered.

"Dave! Where are you? This is Janet. Janet Storie!"

"Janet? It's good to hear from you. It's been more than a couple of years, hasn't it? How is Nick and the kids?"

"We're all fine. Nick and I are on vacation. We're in David!"

"Really?! Why didn't you call and let me know you were coming? Selma's here with me, and CD and Alma just came in an hour ago! I think we ... yes! We have an unused guest room! Come here! I insist, so no shit!"

"Where are you? We're just leaving the airport in a taxi. The driver knows you and this is his phone."

"Let me talk to him. You're about a mile from my place."

Janet handed the phone to the driver. They talked a minute, then he said they'd be right there. He looked around and took a side road after another minute and pulled up in front of a rather nice large house with a steel grate fence. Nick said Dave was doing very well, indeed! The books must be selling. That place had to cost a grand a month, even though Panamá prices were a lot less than Florida. Maintenance and maid service cost an arm ... no, Selma was there. Expensive, no matter what.

"I think about three hundred a month. It *is* expensive, but it's a big house," the driver said.

Dave came out the gate with a woman who looked familiar. She was probably a movie star or something. Nothing surprised them with Dave.

Selma came out with them, then a man he recognized, CD Grimes. The woman must be his wife. She was supposed to be a beauty, and this one was certainly that!

CD chatted with the driver, who took the bags out of the trunk and Nick paid him. It was a dollar and a quarter. They didn't go all the way to downtown. Nick gave him two dollars and they went to the house. Selma, CD, and Alma were waiting on the porch and were introduced.

"Nick Storie. I've heard a lot about you. JK and Tony and Shirley are friends."

"We go places together now and then. To Jim's place on the island out of Naples. We all go to concerts sometimes. The guys from Not So Hard Times play the area, so we all go. Lonnie goes with us a lot, and Serena, his wife.

"I guess you've heard of Lonnie Micks."

"He's as beautiful a man as exists," Janet said. "They had a baby who's going to be so handsome it scares you!"

Alma and Selma agreed. Alma said she was sick of hearing man talk, so the girls would go inside and gossip about them.

"We're going to head for the mountains in a couple of days," Dave said. "CD is an orchid nut. I don't think you're interested in them, are you, Nick?"

"Not really. I think they're pretty, but I'm not into flowers.

"Janet and I have a free vacation on a big mobster, so we thought we'd come here where you said it's so perfect."

"Which one?" Dave asked.

"Artie Doniletti. He and Greco insisted. We're to watch the budget and not to spend more than a million a week."

"Doniletti? I've had some contact with him. He's not the big bad mobster he used to be. The bunch have gone pretty much legit," CD said. "He did the country a favor when he got the Comptons out of Georgia!"

"Yes. Pancho was behind that," Nick agreed.

"How is Pancho?" Dave asked. "I've lost touch with a lot of the people from Florida. We still communicate about three times a year."

"He's a proud father for the second time. He's a very popular figure in South Florida."

"Pancho DeGullio? The most powerful drug lord in the world until you showed he did it all on bluff?" CD asked, grinning.

"He's still the most powerful person in the world when it comes to mobs. They're scared shitless of him!" Dave said.

They talked for another hour, then Clint came by to be introduced. He and Nick seemed to hit it off as well as he and CD had.

Nick was an observer. He was damned good at analyzing a person. CD was sure of himself to an extent that sometimes crossed the line into arrogance. Clint was more a "Go with the flow" type. Nick had been forced, in a few of his cases, to be pragmatic. CD was more the type who would solve a case and pass the responsibility to the courts or whatever. Dave was in some other world.

Nick Storie was a lucky man. He had the best wife in the world and a job he loved and two kids people considered geniuses (he didn't) and was able to make friends with even the world's most powerful mobsters, as well as with almost anybody else who would meet him half way.

If this country was as Dave explained he was really going to enjoy this vacation.

Clint got on his boat three days later. CD, Alma, Nick and Janet – along with Dave and Selma, of course – were going to spend the night with him in Cusapín, then Dave, CD and Alma were off for the jungle. Nick and Janet were going to stay with Clint and family for a few days. Selma would go to Bocas Town.

They were all totally delighted with the place. Miles of beautiful Caribbean sand beaches, rain forests, beautiful water, beautiful view, beautiful people who were warm and friendly. Nito and Nicole came to greet them from the house and to help carry their things. They were introduced and Janet said they were as handsome as Lonnie's kids. CD, Alma, Selma and Nick knew what she was talking about, as did Dave, who said they would see why in a minute. Selma grinned.

They went to the house, where Tyna was laying out a delicious feast of native dishes. She was a stunningly beautiful woman. Indio, with long thick shiny hair to below her waist.

While Janet was far more than an average beautiful woman, Alma was blond and, as Dave stated, one of the most beautiful women in the world. The contrast with the dark woman who was one of the most beautiful women in the world was startling.

They immediately decided they were friends. All of them. They chatted in Spanish and English and were surprised that Nito and Nicole spoke almost unaccented English as well as perfect Spanish and Ngobe. They could shift from one to the other with ease. Dave, Selma and Nick could speak almost as well, except Nick didn't know Ngobe, of course, but preferred to stay with one language, as did Selma. They would have to stop to consider words when they were mixed. CD spoke some Spanish, but was not fluent.

They went around the town and the area. Alma kept finding orchids she'd never seen, as did CD. Nick and Janet couldn't care less about orchids, but were fascinated with the thousands of parrots and two kinds of monkeys. They took a lot of pictures of people and the area. CD said he was glad he brought two dozen memory chips for the cameras. They were going to fill one 8 gig chip before they left Cusapín!

Two little boys and a little girl, all about five or six years old, came along the beach and were greeted. Nito brought them to the house to be introduced. After about twenty minutes they said they were going to go back home. They had been curious about the gringas. Everybody said there was one who was blond and as beautiful as a movie star, most of whom were ugly, except for the makeup and false boobs. Tyna knew the joke, Alma looked a little surprised and nervous, Janet caught it pretty fast. Selma winked at Tyna.

"They're saying you're actually beautiful, while movie stars have to paint on the beauty. It's because none of us wear makeup, isn't it?"

"Yes," Tyna replied. "Only the whores in Chiriqui Grande wear makeup. It makes them look artificial."

"But these are only little children! What do they know of whores?" Alma asked.

"They know about life and people and nature," Clint explained. "Where in the United States would three five and six year old kids be walking alone on a beach – or even in a park – a kilometer from home?"

"Careful! There are perverts in any society," CD warned. "They can't always control themselves."

"Not here," Tyna said.

"How can you be sure?" CD asked.

"Because they'd be dead," Nicole answered. "They don't get counseling and excuses here."

"I read about that in some of Dave's books," Nick put in. "After you're of age, you do what you want. Until then, it's the strongest law on the comarca."

"Yeah! I have to wait until I'm twelve to get molested! Bummer!" Nicole said. "I wish I was a boy. They can get molested anytime they say it's alright."

Nick was amused. Dave, Selma, Tyna, and Clint didn't seem to pay any attention to it. Alma and CD were shocked. Janet seemed mildly surprised.

"Ah! So you're the one in the states who bought one of my books!" Dave said. "You been screwed yet, Nito? You're nine, so you should be having a little fun now and then."

"I didn't like it. I mean, it wasn't bad, but I don't like it. Santos and Rubio like it. I suppose when I'm on the other end of the stick I'll like it."

"Santos and Rubio are your age?" CD asked.

"No. Santos is eleven and Rubio is twelve. They can get off. At least, Rubio can. I don't know about Santos, but he's more gay."

"I don't believe we're having this kind of crazy conversation!" Alma cried. "Clint, he's your *son*! You don't even seem concerned that he was raped?!"

"I wasn't raped. Ton ... a friend wanted to and I wanted to see what it was like, so I said okay. I didn't like it and he only did it one other time when we were playing and it was part of the game, so I agreed by getting in the game."

"They know more about sex at six than I did at sixty," Clint said. "Everyone's done that kind of thing. They just don't lie about it here. They know it's just part of growing up. If someone actually raped one of my kids they'd die a very slow and horrendous death, I flat guarantee."

"CD is probably the only male here who was never molested, but he had a unique life. His grandfather was one of the most famous private detectives in the states and his great grandfather was a billionaire. If anyone touched him they had no chance of surviving more than a couple of hours," Dave said. "Until I came here there weren't ten people who knew half the things I did except the ones I did it with. Here, so what? I'm no different than most of them."

"You've never denied that you tend to be bi," Selma said. "I think I'll go back to Las Tablas tomorrow when you go wandering off in the jungle. I was going to Bocas, but it'll be so cheap and gaudy after here."

Selma had a nice place in Las Tablas, on the Pacific. The conversation changed to other things and they sacked out about midnight.

In the morning they decided to go their separate ways, so everyone crowded into Clint's boat to head for Chiriqui Grande. They would spend an hour or so there, then CD, Alma, Dave and Selma would take Clint's car to David. Nick and Janet would go back to Cusapín.

They were almost to the docks in Chiriqui when Clint got a call. Tyna answered and said it was their old friend from Bocas, Sergio.

"Yo, Sergio! You're back in Bocas or still in David?"

"Bocas. Clint, I don't have much time, but there's a murder that I want to ask your help with. It's out of my league, what with gringos and Germans and Canadians mixed up in it."

It was on speaker. Dave smirked and said this was a great time to find a puzzling murder!

"Who was that? Dave?" Sergio asked. "This is weird enough for him!"

"I'm almost to Chiriqui Grande now. I have company, but I'll try to get to Bocas. I'll call when I grab a bus."

"What the hell?!" Dave exploded. "Take your car! *We'll* take a bus! Christ!"

"You've never seen Bocas, so we can take an extra day and all go there," Clint suggested.

"Tyna will go back home. Selma and I will take a bus. The rest can go on to Bocas in Clint's car," Dave suggested.

"I'll go back to Cusapín with Tyna," Janet said. "I've spent as much time as I care to in Key West, and everyone says Bocas Town is just like Key West."

They agreed to that. Clint said he would be there soon. He was going to take Janet and Tyna to Cusapín, Dave and Selma would take the car, and he would take the boat to Bocas with a couple of famous detectives. The three of them should be able to solve a little murder in two minutes!

They tied to the dock. Omar was there and was going back to Cusapín in a couple of hours. Janet had never been in a cayuca, so Tyna would take her with Omar and Clint and Nick and CD and Alma could go on to Bocas in the boat.

"I've had enough of Key West, myself," Alma said. "I think I'll go with Dave and Selma to David. I like it there. If you get tied up with a case here I can go with Dave to look for orchids. It's what I'm here for!"

"We can go to Fortuna in the areas we didn't go to the past couple of days. It's been a couple of years and I'd like to see what's been changed up there," Dave agreed. "So! You three master detectives can divide your murder into three parts and see who solves it."

Clint tied to the police dock to ask for Sergio, who wasn't there. He would be back in an hour or so. Clint went around to his place on Saigon Bay. He was tying to his deck when his next door neighbor, Judi Lum, a very attractive Oriental woman who was the best person Clint ever found for getting information, came onto her dock. He introduced everyone and found that Judi hadn't been able to learn anything about the murder. It was a man from Belgium, Hans Borker. He had been killed back by Sixth Street. They thought it was a mugging, but nothing fit. All she heard was that a couple of Canadians and two gringos and a German had some kind of deal that they were arguing about. They all seemed to hate each other and everyone was blaming everyone else for their problems.

"They kept mentioning the tongs, so I imagine they crossed Mama Chiang and are in hot water."

Mama Chiang was the reputed head of the most powerful tong in Panamá. She lived on Isla Colón out past the bluffs in a big house on the water where illegal Chinese were suspected of being brought in.

"Damn!" Clint said. "Sergio didn't say the Chinese were involved! That makes it mean and probably unsolvable!"

"Oh, he doesn't know. I heard that while I was talking with Travis and Yveth."

That was part of Judi's value. She innocently talked about things with people and would drop a word or name in passing, act like she couldn't care less, and would get all kinds of information it would take days for Clint to find. He probably would never have learned the Chinese were involved without that.

"I'd like to dig a bit for you, but I have to be in Santiago tonight, so it's up to you."

She had a taxi waiting, so left.

"Seems we're on our own with something I'd have avoided if I'd known," Clint complained.

"It does make it interesting," Nick replied.

"I can get information about almost anything through my links with Crane," CD said. "They'll have a lot about your tong in the military files."

"No. We do this on our own. The last thing we want is for the states to intrude here more than they have," Clint said. "They get a hint and we'll have the CIA and God knows who here fucking up things. The voice of experience speaks!"

"I can get information through the mobs, but I'll agree," Nick said.

"I have a few connections with the mobs," Clint said. "They're not in the states.

"We're on our own!"

The three detectives went to the station to speak with Sergio Valdez, the head of the police in Bocas. He met the others and said he'd had a couple of conversations with a Jim Hill and a Marsha Blevins in Naples through the police computer lines. Dave had suggested it. He had also once talked with JK on a special cellular Dave carried to learn how to get something from a locked computer. He'd even talked with a man who was supposed to be the most powerful mob boss in the world, Pancho DeGulio, on that phone!

"It seems Dave knows about everybody," Sergio said. "He's not impressed by money, but will knock himself out if someone wants to help people. Deserving people, not bums because they want to be bums.

"What we have is that a man was killed back by Sixth Street, just across on C. Hans Borker. Brest Belgium. He's traveling with five people who are in some kind of business deal. They refuse any information, but I hear they were asking about purchasing land on the water out from town. More toward Drago.

"They don't seem to like each other.

"There are two from Canada, Robert Healey and Keith Stoner. Alberta.

"There are two from the states. George Billings and Harry Stine. Galveston and Los Angeles.

"There is one from Germany Gustav Kroner. Hamburg.

"They have been here for less than a week. They were arguing a lot, but no one knows what the subject of the arguments were. They argued in German.

"I've checked as much as I can in the time. Borker was involved with some kind of illegal importation problem in Germany. Healey and Stoner were in a tourist ship deal between Canada and Japan. Billings and Stoner were in farming in California and Texas.

"Kroner, there's no information. It may be an alias and he might carry a false passport. If it is, it's good! Maybe an altered stolen passport.

"He was killed with a garrote, but was also stabbed in the left side. Nothing was removed from the body that we have learned of.

"That's what we have."

"Okay. Sixth Street and behind are the bad part of Bocas Town," Clint said. "There are a number of people living there who came from Colón. I think you'll know what Colón is."

"Transportation and farming. They're moving some-thing," Nick suggested. "Colón? I'd say drugs."

"No evidence of such," Sergio replied.

"Whatever," CD said. "I heard of some uranium being smuggled out of here a couple of years ago."

"It's tied in with agriculture, as a guess," Nick argued. "That would be drugs, first, or something that it would be illegal to take out."

"A new orchid species?" CD wondered. "That *Phragmipedium kovachii* from Peru would have made several people millionaires if they hadn't been caught. Dave's discovered several new species here and there's *bessae* that's very much on that order here. He found a *Sobralia* that's new. *Scaphyglottis* and *Epidendrums*.

"You have *Encyclia cordigera* here. If it was dis-covered in this day and age it would be worth millions."

"Dave discovered an *Anthurium* that got a few people shot. He was almost one of them," Sergio said. "Believe it or not, those people would kill each other for the right to name the thing!"

"He sent Alma a couple of seeds. We have them growing in the intermediate house," CD said, nodding in agreement. "I have an idea for an approach to this. Let's spend a day or two, each with his own method. We can find what's behind it and go from there. If we establish motive we should have it pretty well solved."

They all agreed. Clint and Sergio would fill Nick and CD in on local things. He took them to the Golden Grill and introduced them to several of the local characters. They went their own ways from there.

CD left the Golden Grill and went to the house to use Clint's computer to contact JK, in Florida. He gave the names of everyone he'd heard about to that point. JK grunted and said he's send to that address as soon as he had anything.

A handsome man named Ben Longstreet came in while he was working. He said he heard Clint was back. He kept an eye on the place for him. He watered the plants when Judi was away.

He didn't know anything except that a tourist was murdered. He didn't get involved in Clint's cases. That could be dangerous.

JK sent that Borker was Borker. He didn't have any information on record because he never did anything. He arranged for people to get jobs internationally the past few years. It was all done through the comps. Mostly higher-end engineers and so forth, but he would handle anything from common labor in the oil fields to cruise ship personnel to business management and up.

Healy and Stoner were into cruise lines and had made some shady deals with second-rate cruises posing as prime.

That could be a connection.

Billings and Stine did contracted agricultural work. They employed a lot of Mexicans and Guatemalans, a percent of whom were illegal and they knew it.

Stine had once gotten involved with a Chinese ring who were suspected of bringing young girls into California and forcing them into prostitution. He left

California and went to Texas, where he seemed legit, if not liked.

He thought for a minute, then called Sergio and said to get him some passport information and send it to him at Clint's house. He needed it right away.

"No," Sergio replied.

"What?"

"That's information that's not in your province to get from me."

"I need it! It could answer a very hard question or two!"

"And?"

"I don't...?"

"I'm supposed to tell you to go fuck yourself if you give orders," Sergio answered, with a laugh.

CD laughed. "Yeah. I tend to do that! How about if I request some passport information?"

"You're at Clint's house. Turn on his computer and go to section three. It's Section PP. It's a direct secure connection. I'll send the things we've received. (CD went to the section on the computer.)

"I was speaking with Sheriff Stewart. He said you're fully qualified and are a deputy in his department and a special state marshal for the grand jury, which you don't believe in. You're used to giving orders. I'm to tell you to fuck off when you do. You don't get bent."

"You called Florida?"

"I check on anyone involved in these things. Clint taught me that!

"Stewart said to tell you your son, another CD, is working for him while he gets his degree, as you know, and that he has solved a case for him. He's not as bigheaded about it as you always are."

The information came onto the screen. They chatted a minute more and CD rang off and studied the information.

Borker was somehow the key, he was sure.

Born in Dulange, Belgium. Attended university in Brest, Belgium. Business management major. Studied criminology as minor. Worked for Silas Dupont one year.

Disappeared until two months ago, when he had his passport certified? Silas Dupont?

CD had heard of Silas Dupont. Borker had been an Interpol agent.

Veddyy inderesdink! He had gotten in with this bunch as an undercover agent, so they were up to something big.

Interpol wasn't into agriculture or drugs, to any extent. They were more art and jewelry ... and there was all that pirate treasure coming from Panamá lately! Clint Faraday was in on a lot of it. That pirate museum on the comarca was eleven billion dollars!

He wanted to discuss a thing or three with Clint!

Nick spoke with people at the Golden Grill. Clint and CD soon left and he stayed. Jim was a very interesting person.

Jim said there was something rather strange and a bit sinister about the whole group where Borker was concerned. They were partners in something that was stepping on the wrong kind of toes.

"I don't know what it is, but that Boko character seems to be very interested in them. He's one of Mama Chiang's men.

"She's reputed to be the head of the tongs here. I wouldn't doubt it.

"Uh-oh. Here comes Tom. Clint despises him. He's one of those people who have some kind of need to top your story, no matter what. He's going to know everything there is to know about the case and he knows everyone involved. It's total bullshit. We let him hang around for amusement. He gets into traps he made."

Nick grinned and nodded. He was introduced to Tom as a cop from Florida.

"What part of Florida? I worked with the police in Tampa for awhile. Investigative department."

"Naples. Homicide."

"Oh, really? Do you know Bill Angeles there? Head of something or other. Worked with him in Tampa before he was transferred."

"Never heard of him except some article in the Police Gazette. We get a kick out of those phony stories they make up."

"Er, ah. Yes. He was embarrassed by all that. I was only there for a few days, so don't know what was going on.

"We have a second rate detective from there living right here. Clint Faraday. Gets involved with the police and interferes with their work, then claims it was him who solved something."

"Clint? I'm staying at his places here. He's respected all over the world. He's a lot of things, but you're the first one I ever heard who called him second rate. Sergio can't say enough good about him! Same was true in David. Tonio, head of violent crimes unit, said Clint solved a couple of things for him."

He was trying to think of everyone Clint and Dave had mentioned.

"Silvio, in Chitre, said he really got a big one solved there. It ended up with him getting a million dollars or something. Basilio, jefe on the comarca, says anything they get, they turn over to him because he's practical and thinks like the rest of his people.

"Clint's proud to be declared a Ngobe because of all he's done for them.

"How can you call anyone like that second rate?"

"Oh, no! It's a joke between us! He says I'm a pain in the ass and I say he's second rate! It's just a joke!"

"Well, he's right, at least," Jim said. "Why didn't you ever tell us about Tampa?"

"Er, I, uh, hmm."

"I'd like to chat, but I'm helping Sergio with that Borker murder," Nick said. "Some vacation! It's like I showed up at the station on time this morning for an assignment!"

"Oh, yes. That guy who crossed his partners or something. I'd think that one was cut and dried! One or all of them did it!"

"Oh, probably. I have to establish motive. These kinds of things are usually among people from the same place who know each other. That's that little weird group. I have to find what they're up to."

"Setting up money laundering for the mafia in California. I'd think that was obvious," Tom said, condescendingly.

"Then why the two from Canada and the German?" Nick asked.

"Er. Spread it out so no one suspects. That's why they always argue. So us people will think they're not working together."

"And why is Boko getting into it?" Jim asked.

"Why, er, Boko? Because Mama Chiang wants to run all that."

"Mama Chiang is into laundering?" Jim asked. "That's some news! Smith and Niko were arguing with that Stine person. They're all tangled with Mama Chiang."

"Anders, too," Tom said, leaning closer across the table. "I saw them day before yesterday on the ferry dock when it came in. I was wondering why they were all there. I think, now this is a guess, there was something that came in on that ferry that they all wanted.

"See, if they had some kind of shipment that Mama Chiang found out about, she would be the one to try to grab it.

"I do know they almost got into it!"

Jim nodded the least bit at Nick. "I heard about that. It was them and Mama Chiang's boys? Not them and Anders?"

"Anders wasn't even there by then! He was sitting in the Pirate when I went by ten minutes later!"

Jim raised an eyebrow and nodded. This was actual information.

The subject changed and Nick said he had to go.

He had something, but what was it?

He went to the China to get some things for the house. He looked around at the various stores and noted they were all Chinese. He remembered walking past several stores. All the food stores and a lot of the other almacenes were owned by the Chinese!

He walked up and down all the streets of Bocas Town and out toward Saigon Bay. All the food stores were Chinese. Most of the restaurants were Chinese.

Nick thought, just maybe, Mama Chiang was a lot more than a bystander.

Clint grinned as he left the Golden Grill. Tom was waiting in the park for him to go so he could go over and make a big impression on the gringo. Nick was going to get more information about everybody than he could believe, and all of it bullshit.

Well, Jim would warn him.

He went to the station to ask about the people, knowing Sergio would have all that the police network could find about them. While he was there he found that CD was at the house using the computer when he called Sergio. He told Sergio to tell him to fuck off if he got orders. He listened to Sergio's end of the conversation and read the information being sent. He came to the same conclusion CD had about Interpol, so called Manolo, an agent for that and a couple of other international police agencies. All he found was that Borker wasn't working with art, jewels or drugs.

He contacted Manny Matthews, actually Marko Bocinni, a major mob boss from California who had gone legitimate and was living on Isla San Cristóbal where he could raise a family who wouldn't be ashamed of what Pops did to get his money, even though it was Manny's father who ran the mob like a mob.

The story was that Bocinni was living on a private island in the Mediterranean. He handled the business through computers. He was still powerful and could get information no one else could.

Borker, nothing.

Healey, a few cheap cons.

Stoner, ditto.

Billings, ditto.

Stine, ditto, except he tried to get into prostitution with the wrong group in California. Manny had been "instrumental" in closing down the connections to China.

Kroner was a question mark, but was probably just a schmuck who never did anything to get attention of anybody.

They certainly weren't into money laundering. That was ridiculous. They had no more than a bare minimum financing, none from anyone who would need another laundering scheme.

Judi reported they had some kind of argument with Boko. He was muscle for Mama Chiang and wouldn't have connections with anyone from anywhere else, so what was that about?

"Clint, Esteban said he saw Anders talking with Niko and Boko and Kroner. That could mean something. He aid they seemed to be arguing. Anders was heard to say someone was going to end up fish bait."

"I've heard one tale too many about Mama Chiang's boys. I think I'll go talk to Anders. He's on and off with Chiang, so maybe he'll let something slip.

"I just can't picture anything where Mama Chiang and that bunch could be getting at cross purposes because of ... or maybe I can! But *how*?"

He decided to look up Anders, who ran a sort of halfassed water taxi that catered to private deals. He would bring in people who weren't supposed to be there and no one would know they were there, where the legitimate taxis took the required ID information.

Anders had a little office that was on the porch of his house on Fifth Street. He would loan money at eight percent – per week. He would lend you ten percent value on cameras and cell phones and computers. If it was found they were stolen, it wasn't his fault! He wasn't required to ask for receipts on personal items, such as the nine cell phones a local bum brought to him. If three were reported stolen, he would be very happy to return them to the owners! He wasn't a fence! He would make the bum return any of the money he hadn't drunk up yet.

That way he got nine fifty dollar cell phones for thirty bucks. He returned three of them, so he had three hundred bucks that he spent thirty dollars on.

"Heard you had a row with that bunch of wannabe something-or-others," Clint said, after chatting for a minute about the less than average surfer bunch this year. Clint said too many were getting ripped off for cameras and phones and computers and wouldn't come back anymore. It was getting as bad as Costa Rica.

"Phftt! Never-will-bes. Idiots! Think they can bring in girls and open a casino on maybe ten thousand dollars. The damned license for the casino would be fifty grand! Idiots!"

"They want to run girls? None of the guys here would give them a second look!"

"Gringas and Suizas and Alemanias. They really think anyone here would pay those prices when you can get a girl on the street for fifteen? Idiots!"

"Amos said they wanted to get their hands on old Indio pottery and such, and pirate treasure, but everyone thinks there's an unending source of pirate treasure here."

"There is for the comarca! More than ten billion dollars worth! I wish I could figure a way to get my hands on a few little things. I could retire!"

"Yeah. They went to all the places on the maps and found out that most of it was found a long time ago. Most of it was in other places. If it wasn't for the international publicity it got this government would send in soldiers and take it."

"Yeah. They say I'm a corrupt crook. Didn't they even look at the damned government here? I'm an amateur!"

They chatted for a minute more, then Clint went to the ferry dock. Smith was there. He was a big black who did things for anyone who would pay.

He refused to talk. Period.

CD, Nick, and Clint met at his house just before sundown. Earl and Ben came with food. They were neighbors and good friends who were chefs for gourmets.

After eight o'clock Earl and Ben went into town and the three detectives sat to compare what they had found.

Borker was an agent for Interpol. He wasn't working on jewels, art, drugs, or anything else that Interpol specialized in. It was probable that the others had tumbled and he died as a result.

They had no idea what the bunch was up to. It didn't have anything to do with artifacts or pirate treasure, except as a possible sideline for one or two of them.

They weren't connected. It wasn't about money laundering, but could have been. The idea was to open a casino and launder through it the same as hundreds were doing already. They would be crowded or run out of that in a week.

There might be some connection with Mama Chiang, but she wasn't into laundering money, except through what was an obvious ruse.

Healey and Stoner were in moving people, but that could translate into cargo on cruise ships.

Billings is a nobody with some agricultural ties. Stine is, too, but was caught in a sick scheme to bring in prostitutes. Check on that. There was a hint of that kind of thing.

Kroner was a big question mark.

"Okay. That's general and overall. Now we add our little finds to it," Clint suggested. "I found that Mama Chiang is definitely involved somehow."

"I see a possible connection to something that would explain the agricultural end and possibly even the transportation end," Nick said. "I had a couple of early cases that were based on genetically engineered things. One was poisonous plants and one was about foods that could be grown in salt water.

"I don't suppose that would be here, though. A scientist and the military in the states were behind the first case and Israelis were behind the second. Zionists."

"I've had a case where genetic insertions were used," Clint said. "It could be, but I don't see how that could include others."

"I think maybe it's a scheme to get your pirate ship's treasures, somehow," CD said. "Not really, but it's the only suggestion I've had that makes sense."

"When we add it up, it contains agriculture, Interpol, and transportation," Clint said. "There's something we don't have."

"It also contains Mama Chiang. We have to find everything she's into to know where the real truth lies," Nick argued. "I can't help but think she's behind all the rest.

"What's she into, Clint?"

"Well, her reputation is that she imports a lot of Chinese. They get off the boat with permanent resident or even citizen status and open small businesses. She's managed to take control of the food markets in a big portion of ... and there it is!"

"Yes! It has to be!" CD cried.

"I think I agree," Nick said. "So. Let's add it up with that equation.

"The bunch uses transportation and Interpol about like we thought. We were looking at the agricultural part as being agricultural, but it was about getting workers.

"They were planning to set up some kind of deal where they got people, probably mostly women, here with an indenture scheme. Stine was caught up in that kind of thing in California ten years ago and managed to barely slip out of it. Healey was getting Mexican and Guatemalan illegals jobs.

"Kroner has connections where European and Asian people who are desperate could be used in such a scheme. In higher income positions."

"And Mama Chiang is running that kind of thing. It would interfere with her scheme," CD agreed.

"Borker was about to expose the thing, which would also give Mama Chiang publicity that could shut part of her things down," Clint added. "Now we have to learn who killed Borker. That puts us in a scary position. We're against these amateurs on one side and the tong on the other.

"In the morning I'm going calling on Mama Chiang."

"I'll go calling on the people she was using here," CD said.

"And I'll go calling on our plotters. Particularly the one I think was the brains. Kroner."

They relaxed and had a couple beers. CD asked if Ben was gay.

"Ben? And Earl? Yes. Both of them. They're a couple. Why?" Clint answered.

"I was just wondering. They seem affectionate with each other. I'm getting used to the guys hugging each other and such, but they seemed closer than that."

They discussed the difference in the cultures and sacked out around midnight.

In the morning Clint headed for The Bluffs and Mama Chiang. Niko met him at the gate and said Mama Chiang was expecting him. He went in and was ushered to the veranda, where she was having breakfast. She invited him to join her. He said he'd eaten, but could always use a cup of coffee.

"Well, Mr. Faraday. I've been expecting you since Smith said you asked some questions he wouldn't answer."

"They were about him, not you. The fact he came to you answers some of the questions for me. I was coming because your name and organization were mentioned by a number of people."

She nodded. "My organization?"

"It's simply common knowledge. We don't need to dance around about it. You're offering employment to people who wouldn't have any, otherwise. I may not approve of the fact you make more than they do off of it, but there are probably any number of things about me you wouldn't be able to approve.

"Do you know who Borker was?"

"The dead man? He was an accountant of some sort, according to my sources."

"Then you'd better find better sources. He was Interpol. If you were behind his murder, you've managed to bring an international investigation on that you can't bribe or intimidate."

She stared hard at him for a moment. "I see.

"No, Mr. Faraday, I was not behind his killing. If I were, there would be no body and the crabs several miles out in the Caribbean would be well-fed for awhile.

"I cannot say that no one close to me was involved. That kind of thing can happen when a person thinks he is doing a favor for another person. The road to Hell is cobbled with good intentions.

"Mr. Faraday, I've been greatly curtailed in the import department by the recent amnesty program that showed some people had carried improper identification. We are an intelligent people and they saw they could have amnesty and become truly legal here, meanwhile relieving themselves of paying for being here in the first place. I have had to virtually cease the operation.

"It isn't all negative. I can use a little retirement to rest and enjoy what I've earned."

"Well, I don't suppose you're involved and don't think your help would do anything like that without orders. I'm left with only the ones who knew Borker was Interpol. That would be their own little group."

"Niko did tell me that someone said there is a man here from the world police. He heard about it at the ferry ... never mind. It is rumor."

They chatted a bit. Clint soon headed home. Maybe they could narrow it down to the one who actually killed him.

Or two?

Regardless, Clint wanted all of them out of Panamá. The one who killed an Interpol agent was going to be prosecuted all the way.

CD went down by the ferry dock where he saw Smith talking to Boko. He went to them and introduced himself. He said he was going to find the one who killed Borker.

"You for real, Man?" Smith said, with a sneer. "Ain't nobody here offed the turkey. It were one of his buddies, Man!"

"There was a wire around his neck?" Niko asked. "It wasn't us. We know fifty ways to eliminate people without using more than your hands and feet."

"I heard it was a wire and he got stuck," Smith said. "Getting stuck is an occupational hazard. No wire around the neck. Why both?"

"Why, indeed? So you could say you would never do it that way?" CD replied. "Do you know who he was?"

"He was just a fucking gringo tourist," Smith snarled. "Ain't enough of them getting offed!"

"Then you wouldn't have anyone to rip off. Think about it! Why are you here?" Clint fired back. "A ladron has to have somebody to steal *from*!"

"You got a mouth, Man! Maybe I'll off another one for kicks!"

"Give it a go, hotshit! You've got a body twice my size and a brain ten percent of my size!"

"Stop it! Both of you!" Niko demanded. "I'll kick both your stupid asses!"

CD laughed. "You could probably do it."

"So you'd just shoot me. Hai, karate! Hai, forty five!"

"Do you know who offed him? Really?"

"I don't. Smith might."

"Nah. What you mean, 'Know who he was?' He was nobody!"

"He was Interpol, so they'll come here and tear this place apart if I can't find who killed him first."

"Shit!" Smith said.

"That's about my reaction. Mama Chiang is going to be very upset about this," Niko said. He took out a cell phone and called a number. He said he'd found that Borker was an Interpol agent, that there was going to be trouble. They had to be able to give them the one who killed Borker. He listened a minute, then rang off.

"Mama Chiang already knew it. I'll never know how she always knows everything about anything before anybody else."

CD knew Clint was going to talk to her. He could tell them ... nah!

CD went to find Anders, who had already talked with Clint the day before.

If it was one of this group it would be Boko.

He went to find Boko, who claimed to have been in Changuinola to collect some payments for Mama Chiang the time of the murder.

He would be alibied by someone, CD had no doubt. He thought he could believe it, despite that.

He headed for the house.

Nick stopped at the Grill to say hello. Jim was there, and David and Bob and Aaron.

And Tom, of course. Tom was saying he was going to write a book about this case. He had it figured out. Mama Chiang had him knocked over because he was the brains and was planning to open a little mall over close to the cemetery that would include a casino and bar and stores. He would compete with prices while no one there now ever did. It was about time he wrote another one.

"Oh? You write books? What kind?" CD asked

"Oh, whatever. Things like this case come up. I can almost always figure them out, so I write about it."

"I know a man who writes books here. Dave. He's had more than a hundred fifty published."

"Er, um. Yes. I know him. He's used some of my ideas."

"Oh, come on! Dave thinks you're a total ass!" Bob snapped. "He's already shown you up! Why don't you have the sense to stop while you're ahead?

"CD, was it? Dave marched Tom and several of the rest of us to the internet café at Don Chicho's and looked up his book. It was a vanity press thing that didn't sell a hundred copies, total! Dave's got the first nine pages when you Google or Yahoo! search his name!

"Tom likes to dig a hole and fall into it."

"My book sold the entire first publishing!" Tom protested.

"It was POD! That's one book!" Bob shot back.

Tom got up and stomped off. Jim laughed and said, "Bob thinks about as much of Tom as Clint."

"Yes. I can certainly see why, though something he said did help a lot. About the Chinese and the bunch arguing.

"You found out who Borker was yet?"

"I hear he was FBI, but that was from Tom, so it was nothing like that. We said maybe CIA, but he went into why the FBI is taking over the CIA. He heard it from a personal friend who's head of certain covert operations in the FBI."

"Oh? Tom knows a legal aide on apprenticeship at the FBI offices in Two Eggs, Florida?"

They laughed and said they didn't believe it was anyone that high on the scale.

After a few more minutes Nick went to the Sagitario Hotel to talk with Billings and Healey. They were staying at the cheapest hotel on Isla Colón while they opened a big project?

They didn't know who killed Borker. They had no idea why he was killed.

"He was working with Interpol. Did you know that?" Nick asked innocently. Healey dropped his beer. Billings looked like he'd been slapped with a rotted dead fish.

"I can see you didn't. Bad scene, huh?"

"Oh, God *damn*!" Billings cried. "I should have known Harry would bring in someone to fuck up the works. He's always been a fuck-up! Christ!"

"You've known him far a long time?"

"He came to Galveston about six years ago. He claimed he was working for a company that the FBI raided and he barely was able to show them he wasn't involved. It gave him the idea ... well, that's over now. I just want to get back home and never have to think about this mess again!"

"We're lucky, in a way. We haven't done anything illegal."

"Yet," Nick said. Healey nodded and looked grim.

"Except maybe kill him?" Nick added.

"If we'd known, the last thing we'd do would be bring the damned Interpol down on our heads! Christ!" Billings cried.

Nick could believe that. He eliminated these two. That left three.

He went back and saw Stoner and Stine sitting at The Pirate. He went in and said, "Hi! Just talking with Billings and Healey. They're getting out of here as fast as they can. They didn't know Borker was Interpol and don't want to be around when they come to investigate.

"I guess you'll want to go, too."

Stoner stared and looked like he'd faint. He was suddenly pale and sweating. Stine looked hard and grim.

"So. You killed Borker," Nick said to Stine. "You're the only one who knew Borker was Interpol."

"No. I didn't kill anybody and I'm not the only one who knew. One of our group knew and one Panamanian. I found out about it just before he was killed."

"There's only one more in your group. Kroner. There are things about Kroner that say he didn't kill anybody that way. He's not big enough, for one thing.

"So! Who's the Panamanian?"

Clint thought about it. It only added up one way. He sighed and decided to get it over with.

CD carefully considered what he'd learned. He called Sergio and requested an address and told him why. Sergio would meet him there.

Nick went over what had happened and what he'd heard. It only added up one way. He knew where to go because he'd passed the place while he was walking the town.

Harley Anders saw Clint coming and sighed. He guessed he knew Clint would figure it out.

There comes that CD character. With Sergio? Did Clint really think he would need help?

What the hell! Now that Nick person is coming around the corner! He wasn't holed up with an AK47! They didn't need a SWAT team!

Clint was coming onto the porch and saw Anders staring over his shoulder, so turned. Sergio and CD coming from directly across and Nick coming from the corner. He grinned at Anders. Anders said, "What the hell, Clint?"

"I guess we all figured it at the same time. We were working from the same information. You're the only one who didn't quite fit.

"Why did you kill him, Harley?"

"He was with Interpol. He caught me carrying some pirate stuff to Almirante and stopped me there and said he was going to have me arrested and charged with international commerce in stolen jewels. I figured there was maybe a fifty-fifty chance you would tag one of his buddies he didn't get along with for killing him."

"None of them had anything to do with it?" CD asked. Anders shrugged. "No."

"He was Interpol," Sergio said. "There's no way out."

"I know, " Anders replied. "Can I have tonight to straighten up all this shit around here?"

"If you promise not to run."

"Okay. What time tomorrow?"

"I come on duty at one, so be there then. Bring a toothbrush and all that crap."

"Okay."

"And that was it!" Nick exclaimed. Janet grinned.

"We're a lot more civilized here than in the states," Tyna said. "Clint usually just makes them leave Panamá. We don't need the expense of feeding and housing them for the next twenty years. This one is Panamanian, so we do have that."

"Borker was Interpol. Won't they send him to France or something?" CD asked.

"No. So far as Panamá is concerned, it was a murder to avoid exposure in Panamá and was committed by a Panamanian, so he gets tried and convicted here," Clint said. "The others in that little group will be sent on their sordid ways and declared undesirables, so they can't ever come back. The evidence, particularly against Stine, is already there, waiting for him. Kroner won't ever find any decent employment in Germany again. The rest, I couldn't care less."

"Well, I'll head for David this morning. Alma will be waiting. I'd, personally, prefer to stay right here for the next fifty years or so, but I promised."

"You're welcome to stay as long as you like," Tyna said.

"We're going to stay here for the rest of our two weeks," Janet said, "I hope to be a regular visitor! This place is paradise!"

"You'll have to get used to our ways. Clint especially," Tyna warned. "Clint, go swimming and put on some clothes. We have visitors!"

Clint had forgotten to put on anything. He never did before he had his breakfast and a swim. Nito had come in and was just coming back from the beach. He and Nicole. They would get dressed and go to school.

"I'll run you to Chiriqui Grande, CD. It's no trouble. Really!" Clint said.

"I want to ride the cayuca. It also lets me stay here a little longer."

Clint and Nick went to the water and swam awhile. They waved when Nito, Nicole and CD headed for Cusapín, then when Janet and Tyna went the same way ten minutes later.

"I've never been a nudist before. This is great!" Nick said. Clint agreed. "We're not built any different than anyone else. I'm comfortable like this.

"Tyna left breakfast for us. Janet fits in perfectly here. She's volunteered to help with the cacao this morning. My people feel we all have a duty to the community.

"I'm going to work with preparing a field for frijoles. You can laze around or whatever you like."

"I'll help with the frijoles. As good as these people are to me, I feel like one of you."

Clint nodded. They went to the house, dressed, ate the breakfast, and headed for town.

Nick Storie felt he was the luckiest man in the world!

Clint wondered what was coming next. He really did like a puzzle!

Three detectives retire to a paradise place (Well, one was already there) and unite to try to solve a difficult case.

Contents

The Deal

CD Grimes, PI, billionaire, signed the titulo. Alma, his wife, signed. CD gave Emilio Fuentes the check for one point five million dollars. They went to the caja to pay the notary fee, shook hands, and Fuentes got in his car and left.

"Done deal!" CD said to Alma. "We now own that chunk of paradise!"

"CD, I never really believed there was a perfect place for us. This is it!

"I'm so glad we met Clint and learned about it. I'll miss Dave here, is all. He was half-crazy and weird, but we went all over this place for the orchids. I think I'll have the most complete collection of native orchids of Panamá in the world. He left me the three places he made gardens. I have that place in Calderas for the really high altitude types. The island has a peak at six hundred meters, so the warm and intermediate ones will do very well there. The comarca's two hundred sixty meters away. They'll inherit the place. He has more than eight hundred species there.

"We can live in that house there until we have a place built. I guess you'll want an underground cold house."

"No. We have the place in Calderas. I doubt I'll do a lot more with hybrids of those types. Maybe it would be better to leave those things in the states. We can spend ten lifetimes doing the kinds of things Dave and you were working on. I'm more and more into that."

"Okay. We also have a deal on other things. The business is now in the hands of the kids. They run things without your interference. They learned how to keep on top of the government and all that from you. They aren't interested in the detective bit, so I guess the CD Grimes Detective Agency is another thing of the past.

"CD, I think we've both been able to make a mark on the world. Dave and Clint and the Stories think exactly like we do. We fit together and we fit this place. We've always had a philosophy more like the Indios than what passes for 'normal' in the society we're finally able to escape completely.

"We have to work out some way for Nick and Janet to come here. Clint isn't far a good part of the time. Cusapín is only thirty kilometers away. They both love the country and the lifestyle. Nick has had his fill of the kinds of greedy crime he's worked with. It's too true in the states that it's a ratrace where the rats are winning."

"I've talked with Nick. He's already agreed that he would like nothing better, but he has some kind of hang-up because we can afford this kind of thing and he's a cop with a cop's salary. He'll get the pension and his Social Security and has a few dollars in the bank. I've got Pancho DeGulio and JK convincing him to come.

"I want Pancho to come. He says he'll spend part of his time here, but he can't stay for long. If he's here those gangsters he's reformed would start wondering if they could take over from ... that's not true. Others would move in.

"All our friends will be welcomed. I doubt their psychologies would let them be content with this kind of life.

"Well, I want to talk to Clint while I'm here. This is close. I think he and Tyna would like to live out here. He's getting worried about becoming useless on the comarca, though that won't ever happen. He's almost eighty and in better health and condition than most people in their thirties. His kids have made names for themselves, same as ours and Nick's.

"Cole, Nick's son, is making a big splash in Florida with his forensics research."

"Clint's, Nito, is making a name in police procedures. He's modernized the Policia Nacionál to where most in the states are using his techniques. If it wasn't for the corruption in the courts, this country would be the envy of the Americas! Nicole married an Indio and is making a name in medicine. She's running all those hospitals and clinics Clint and Manny built."

"I'll let you stay here with Tyna and Clint. I'll talk with Clint, then go back to Florida to get things settled and have what you want sent. I won't bring much, myself."

"I made a list and gave it to the kids. It's not a whole lot. The paperwork and that sort of thing is all on flash drives. There's some equipment and a few personal items. It'll be the first time in my life I've moved where I didn't need a convoy to carry the crap! Everything will fit on the plane and you'll have room for four passengers to top it.

"CD, try to make Nick and Janet two passengers, okay? Janet and I click and you and Nick click. All of us click with Clint and Tyna."

"I'll give it a go!"

"Clint, we really would like for you and Tyna to live there at least part of the time. Alma and Tyna get along as well as we do. I'm going to try to get Nick and Janet to come here. Nick's ready to retire. We all think alike on major issues. We've all spent most of our lives setting up others to have something. It's time we had a little bit for ourselves. We've got money up the ass, but not much that really matters.

"I'm speaking mostly for me. You have a life I envy the hell out of. What you always warn about has happened to me. I don't have the money, it has me.

"More than that, I'm talking about Tyna and Janet and Alma. You know they've gone through a lot for us. It's time to give them something back. Money ain't it. They've got more than they know what to do with. Tyna loves this kind of place. It's a lot like the comarca, but without the pressures of the comarca. Alma loves it. It's where she can do the things that she really wants to do. She won't have to run away from anything to do that here. Janet can be in a place where she doesn't have to agonize over her husband being a cop on violence detail. She won't spend her life with the dred of opening the door to find two cops with black armbands who come to break the news to her.

"Okay. Tyna will have fifty Indios living on the island. It's big enough. There are four families living there now. I told them they could stay as long as they like. You know what I mean. We get along very well. Alton has that place and fishes. He can supply us with sea-foods and we'll supply him and family with whatever they need. Berto is already growing cacao and coffee here. And a lot of other things. We'll be totally self-sufficient here."

Clint thought about it. He was seventy nine and in very good health and condition. Tyna was as healthy, but they could both use less pressure. They had made that pressure a part of their lives deliberately, but that was when they were thirty years younger.

"I think I could go for that, but Tyna won't want a fancy house or those kinds of trappings."

"Alma and I are sick of that shit, ourselves. Basic, but comfortable. One room I don't ever have to go into with the things that are likely to come up because of the business and so forth. Alma's happy in a tent in the jungle. I only want a clean comfortable place. I like to sit on the porch and watch the sunrises and sunsets."

"Deal!"

CD's phone rang. He was expecting two calls. This one was from Pancho DeGulio, one of the most powerful people in the world when it came to the mobs – not because of anything he did, but because of what he knew.

"CD here. It's your dime."

"A call costs a quarter, locally. This isn't locally," Pancho replied. "How are things in Panamá?"

"Better than I deserve. I want to ask you for a couple of favors having to do with this place."

"So? Ask!"

"I bought an island on the border of the comarca. I'm moving here with Alma. Clint and Tyna are going to live there. I want you and Nick and your families to move here.

"I know your situation. I know you can't stay long at a time, but I want you to have a place here. Your wife and family can stay, too.

"I want you to convince Nick and Janet. They want to come, but feel they would be out of place. We're all millionaires. We really do want them here. It will be basic. We'll live more like the comarca lifestyle. No greed or materialism and no laying around being a bum. Natural life with natural responsibilities."

"I will see. I think Nick knows he's really the same as you. I'll speak with him."

"I'm coming back to Florida tomorrow. I'd like for you and your family and Nick and Janet to come back here with me."

"I will be unable to come for about two months. Perhaps I can convince Nick to retire and come. The only reason he hasn't retired already is because he would have nothing to do. That isn't a position any of our little group could tolerate. for more than a week."

"We have a deal! Paradise, and we don't even have to die to get here!"

*

Det. Lt. Nick Storie (*) had a method that had worked well for much of his career. He was basically a problem solver. He would locate the point where what he needed to know was, then go there. He wondered how that would affect his new life. He would simply have to find new kinds of problems to solve. He ended up friends with most of the top gangsters in the states. They respected him as a man whose honor was unquestionable. He even ended up friends with many he caught. He might agree with parts of it, but his sworn job was to catch them. What the courts and lawyers did past that point wasn't his decision to make.

"Nick, I didn't say anything. I know it's your decision, but I'm so thrilled we're going to be able to live down there I can't describe it! Alma and Tyna are the very two people in this world I can relate to completely. We think very much alike. We like to do things, even though they're different kinds of things for each of us. Alma wants to tramp all over the jungle, Tyna wants to be with the people on the comarca, I want to write a book! I've wanted to write a book for years and never could get started. Whenever I think of a way, something happens to make me wait another day, then I don't.

"I believe the book won't be so dark, there. Here, it would be about fighting and arguing and doing whatever it takes to accomplish something that would be just plain silly down there. Maybe I can write something worth reading."

"You want to write a book? Too bad Dave's not here anymore. He wrote two or three hundred books!"

"I know. He's where I got the idea."

The caller vibrated. He looked at it.

"Well, I turned in my resignation/retirement today. I get home and get a call.

"My last case assignment for South Station, Naples, Florida! I hope I can solve it tonight so we can start packing in the morning!"

"Yeah, right, and uh-huh!"

He kissed her soundly and headed for his car.

**

Clint Faraday, PI, Retired, (**) was a legwork type with a mind that sought the surest way through a situation. He had also learned to be pragmatic about a lot of things. Things that served well in the USA were just plain silly and extreme here. The older he got, the more he fell into the Indigeno thought patterns about many things.

"Clint! It's Rojelio from Chiriqui Grande!" Tyna called. Clint answered the phone.

"Clint? Que tal? Got a bit of a problem here. I would appreciate your help. It's the kind of thing you're so good at. Two people killed in a traffic accident that wasn't."

"How was it done? Who?"

"Car went over the side just above Cañastas. No skid marks. In neutral. Brakes working. Head wounds not consistent with any surface they might have met. Man and wife. Campbells. Mid-fifties. From Nevada. Tourists. Didn't have much money. No alcohol or drugs.

Staying in Bocas, on the island. Seemed suspicious and were hiding something or from something.

"I studied police procedures under Nito. That's basically what you need? I haven't spent much time on it. It happened last night about seven thirty."

"I'll go to Isla Colón. I'll see what I can see."

***

CD Grimes, PI, (***) was a billionaire who had rejected a lot of the lifestyle of those people in the USA. Most money people were, to him, greedy, empty, boring things. He couldn't divest himself of Crane because of many contracts with the military and government agencies. To simply close down Crane would put three thousand people out of work overnight. He had managed to put most of that on Tony Jacobi, who had, for years, been the real head of Crane.

CD had become famous, in a way, in Florida. He went through the courses about police work and law, was for many years a semi-official deputy sheriff and a state marshal for the grand jury (which he didn't believe had a legitimate place in law in his earlier years). He used his position to have a lot of things done for him. His security clearances and certifications were honestly earned. He believed in what he was doing until it got so out of hand.

He was considered pompous and arrogant until you got to know him. It was his method. He convinced himself that, without any doubt whatever, he would solve any case he took. So far, most of that was successful.

The world had changed radically in the past fifty years. CD had changed little. His ideas clashed with what was considered as acceptable now. Money had bought out honor in much of the world. He was an honorable man, as were Nick and Clint. That was their real connection.

CD got out of the Jeep at the Crane plant to go to his son's office. A woman was just leaving, so he went in.

"Hi, Dad! So you're really going to abandon us with this mess?"

"Yeah, CD. I had Tony to run things until you were ready. I've said before that you would be smart to find someone like him to screw things up!"

"Tony Jacobi screw things up? You're joking, of course! He spent half his time unscrewing things you'd made a mess of!"

Well, you can work out a system to screw things up. JK can undo it. He's the one who runs things, anyhow."

"He had two senators and two reps here to whine and beg. I don't know what it was about, but they made some kind of deal where that bunch retired for personal and health reasons. I guess their replacements will be as bad or worse.

"Oh! Fred Hampton called. He wants you to call him as soon as you have a spare moment."

"Fred Hampton?"

"He said he knew you from the orchid society. I suppose it will be about that."

"You have to see to all those things now, you know. I'm not about to take three acres of greenhouse orchids to a place where you see them naturally, no matter where you look."

"Sis will handle that. She's into them. I'm not. My brother is, more than me."

CD nodded and took the phone to call the number CD (His son) gave him. Hampton answered. He said CD was known as a detective in murder cases. There was a murder in his family. The police wouldn't even investigate it!

"I only have a day or two, but I'll look into it. Meet me at Sancho's Mexican in thirty minutes? It's lunch time. I want to tell all of them there goodbye. I'm moving out of the states."

*

"Hi, Larry. What's up? You called for me to assist?" Larry Feng was a good cop. Nick had arranged for him to go into police work twenty years ago. He worked several stations and was now head of violent crimes, South Station. Nick had turned down the position four times. He wasn't the administrator type, and that's what the position required.

"It might not be much, but you can usually spot things that everyone else will miss.

"Remember, back in about ninety four, when you introduced me to Greco? That crazy Mexican woman who wanted to establish a chain of whorehouses here?" (Nick Storie book 13: *Trigger Happy/ Strange Fish*)

"Lord, yes! That was something. It could have ruined the Olympic Games in Atlanta!"

"Greco called me. He asked if you could check into something for him here. It has to do with that. Candida got out of the pen after serving the twenty years. The one you called Jojo didn't get any reduction. Not a good prisoner.

"She got out three days ago. She was sent directly to Mexico. Mexico wanted Jojo extradited there. He was supposed to be a witness ... well, who cares. He was to testify against her. He was being transferred to Miami. He had to come here to get an extradition order in the place where he was convicted."

Page 65

"And he was hit," Nick finished.

"Pancho will know all about it. You can talk to him, nobody else can. Greco may be able to tell you something."

Nick sighed deeply and picked up the phone to call Greco, in Detroit, who conferenced with Artie Doniletti in New York. Mo Jefferson, the other major crime lord (now gone legitimate) Nick knew, had died of cancer two years ago. Julia Bocci, now Julia Doniletti, was in the hotel business and had been involved in that case.

"What's the skinny, Greco?" Nick asked when all were on the line.

"Short and sweet. Candida's out. Jojo was hit. He would tie her ass in a knot in Mexico. Who and how arranged? We do not want that one around, even as close as Mexico. None of us want to go back to the old days. We don't arrange hits anymore, or it would be a non-issue already."

"It will be someone she met in the pen. It was arranged there, probably. Where was she held?"

"Raiford. Artie checked that out."

"She had three people she was palsy with in the can," Artie said. "One is still there. She couldn't arrange anything. One is in Texas, and one is in Mexico as her guest. She's there."

"She could arrange it like we're doing. Talking on the phone. Whoever did it was damned professional, I'm guessing, if they hit him while in custody," Nick replied. "There's one person who might have a direction. I'll call Pancho.

"Guys, I'm retired from the police thing here. I'm moving to Panamá. There's a retired detective from Florida, the Tampa area, who's got a fantastic place where we'll all live. On an island in the Caribbean. It's pure paradise!"

They all wished him well. They would stay in touch. If they could arrange a vacation they'd visit.

Nick called Pancho. They discussed the case. Pancho would get a request for information out. They then talked about the Panamá place.

Nick thought about this case, sighed again, and sent a request for information to the holding facility. He got a quick response. Jojo was hit from a distance with a high-powered rifle shot. One inch above the right ear. Definitely a professional job.

He then used the computer to get all information he could about Candida's stay in Raiford. They had it ready because of the hit and it came in fast. He saw the three closest friends and that they were immediately checked. None could have done it, not to mention they weren't the type who would.

Visitors. One name seemed familiar. Sam Levin. Two visits, both in the last month.

Sam Levin and hits. What about that case where the Cuban woman was hit that way? Wasn't he suspected? Didn't he get a conviction ... it was his girlfriend. Her name was Gina Samosini. She was doing twenty to life.

But he was a suspected hit man.

Nick called Raiford to ask about Gina Samosini. She was there. She had some contact with Candida. Not much.

One short conversation would be enough.

Nick called Pancho and asked about Levin and Samosini. There was a silence, then, "Nick, you never fail to amaze me! I would never connect Levin with

Candida, but his girlfriend ... and he visited her at Raiford. When?"

"Twice. Last month on the twenty second and on the twenty eighth. Candida already knew she was going to get out soon and be sent to Mexico. She could have fifty ways to learn Jojo was going to squeal on the deal."

"His address is listed on the visitor's list. See if he was anywhere he could have done it. If he was, case solved!"

Nick soon hung up and called Raiford one last time. Levin was in Sarasota. An hour away by car or bus on I-4.

Nick called in to Larry to say to check on where Sam Levin was at the time of the hit, find anyone who can say he was in that area, arrest him, and contact Mexico. Levin could make a deal to testify in Mexico that Candida paid him to eliminate the person who would make her conviction there a definite thing or he could face M-1 charges here. His choice.

"We're going to miss you and your connections here!" Larry said. "One of them will always know about anything vaguely related to their business."

"Not in this case, Lare. They didn't know where to look. If I hadn't had two unrelated cases where certain of the people were involved I wouldn't have seen the connection. It would have to go to the unsolvable file: Mobs."

"Nobody else would have seen the connection, even if they were involved in those two cases. You would. That's why you were so good."

"I still am. I just don't want to spend the rest of my life doing this. I'm going to Panamá."

Larry grinned and gave him the old one finger salute.

**

"Jelio, I have to know a hell of a lot more about the Campbells. I've checked them out here in Bocas. There are some huge gaps in what I've learned, so far. It smells like a WP deal or something. The Campbells, these, didn't exist six years ago. I can't find much with the system that's worked so well for the past fifteen years. That means someone has gone to one hell of a lot of trouble to erase information from the web.

"It's not possible to erase it all. I have to check a few things. One thing will be certain, if it's WP or not. They weren't from Nevada. They'd probably never been there. My connections to the old mobs don't have a clue.

"I'd say to forget it if some things hadn't been mentioned. Things that involve Panamá. Things that could involve the comarcas. Things that could involve ... a lot of things.

"Jelio, they were very damned important to something. It could be something very nasty.

"I'll try to find the one who offed them, just to be able to find who hired him. I have a very good idea who that might have been, among three.

"You said the transmission was in neutral? Prints on the shift knob?"

"Wiped clean. Another reason we know it was no accident."

"Then I'm ninety percent certain I can find the one who did it. I think I can get information from him. I have a lever."

They talked a few minutes, then Clint took his boat to Almirante, where he asked if Tigre was back there.

No. He didn't think he would be. He asked that so he could throw some other names around that would make others think he didn't know who he was after.

"Evan Roberts? He went back to Costa Rica."

"Martín? Last I heard he was in Las Tablas – which thrills the shit out of people there, I suppose."

"Anderson? He's around somewhere. Chiriqui Grande last week."

"Arauz? Benito? Darien."

So. It was who he thought. Anderson. He had money now, so would be in David at the casinos.

Clint took his boat to Chiriqui Grande, got his car and headed for David. Anderson had been there a couple of nights ago, then had left. Probably to Panamá City.

Clint got a flight. Anderson had stayed in David, done the job, and took the money to head for the city and the big casinos – where he'd lose it all.

Clint checked into the Hotel California. Anderson would hit the casinos at about ten if he held to his pattern.

Eleven fifteen. The Grande Game. He was at the bar with his hooker for the night. Clint went to say he needed a quick word, then he could get back to his girlfriend.

Anderson knew him from a case before. A case where he had sent two people over the side of a mountain in a car with the transmission in neutral. Due to who they were, he let it slide, but had warned Anderson that he left prints on the gearshift knob. As soon as he heard the knob was wiped clean, he was sure it would be Anderson.

"Who paid? That's all I have to know."

"I don't know. Two grand up front, then two more when it was done. Voice on the phone. Money appeared by my door in a dirty paper bag when I got home, then inside an open window on the floor when I did the job.

All I got was a note that they would look me up if they needed more contract work."

"Got the note?"

He reached in his pocket and handed Clint a typed note: *Aces, Pedro. I will look you up if and when more contract work is needed.*

"Thanks. Get back to your whore before some other mark gets her eye."

"Thirty others here. Like I give a shit?"

"They call you Pedro?"

"No."

Clint grinned and went out. He went back to Chiriqui Grande in the morning. He told Rojelio it was a professional job and there wouldn't ever be enough evidence to convict anybody.

He was a bit curious. He would check into it some more. Later. He went back to Cusapín.

***

CD looked over the bunch at the restaurant. That was Hampton to the side. He went over. Hampton waved to the other seat. He ordered tamales and tacos.

"What's it about?"

Fred shrugged. "My cousin was shot in the back of the head. George Bender. He wasn't using drugs, but it was execution style. He didn't even know any of those kinds. He was into religion, much more than I ever was. The police say it was obviously a drug-related execution, proven by the way it was done. They say all they can do is hope somebody says something, then they don't have much chance of getting a conviction.

"We all tried to tell them he was the last person on Earth who would ever have anything whatever to do with drugs. They said a lot of people have that rep-

Page 71

utation. If it had been true, he wouldn't be executed that way.

"Don't you wish cops were actually like those on CSI and New York Law or whatever?"

CD shook his head. He agreed that law was becoming more and more an unfunny joke. Drugs were blamed for everything.

"Tell me as much as you know about what he was doing and where and with whom."

"He was into evangelical work, which means he would knock on your door and ask if you knew Jesus was your lord and savior and that kind of thing. He would try to convert you to the Church of Absolute Truth So There! or whatever.

"He really was honest with it. It was what he believed. I shouldn't put him down for it. He was the type you wanted to toss off the property, but no one would want to hurt him. I just don't get it!"

"He would go into neighborhoods and knock on doors. That kind. He was devout in his beliefs.

"Do you know which neighborhoods he was working lately?"

"Those closest to where his church was, I would imagine. He would sometimes go out to the island. He said there were more people there who were lost than in most areas. Most of those had a maid to answer the door and tell him to take a hike, so he didn't ... he did say he saw something on Ana Mariah that troubled him deeply. Something about corrupting the youth, leading them astray. He saw something. A lot of lost souls who needed direction. He was going to speak with them about it or report it to someone or something."

"When?"

"About ten days ago. It was toward the causeway, I know. He said it was an ostentatious shrine to Satan.

"Yes! He said there was a yacht at the dock that shouldn't be there and that a lot of teenagers were partying on it! There was some fancy Italian car in the drive and a lot of BMW's and Lexuses and those kind of things."

"A yacht that shouldn't have been there? That could mean something. Did he say why it shouldn't have been there?"

There was a pause. "I'm trying to remember. We all sort of tune him out when ... a leader ... no, a ... politician of some sort, I think. I may be pissing up a rope, but I think it was something like that."

"I'll look into it, but won't have much time. I'm moving out of the states. If I can find anything I know which cop to have go after it. I can't promise anything except that I *will* look into it."

They talked a bit more. CD suggested his cousin had probably confronted the wrong kind of people. If they thought he was threatening them, exactly what had happened would happen.

They had the meal, CD told his friends there he was leaving, then went to the old Jeep he liked to drive. He was a billionaire who rode around in a restored WWII Jeep! And piloted his own six seater jet.

He drove out to the causeway and found what had to be the house. After talking to several near neighbors' housekeepers and yardmen, he knew which house. Two had seen a yacht at the dock more than once. Yes, there were a lot of teenagers hanging around. The people in the house didn't have any children. There was booze if not worse. Draw your own conclusions.

One said the name on the yacht was Dare2Bea.

A check of the records said the Dare2Bea was leased to a state attorney's aide.

CD asked, "A state attorney's aide makes enough to lease a yacht?"

"Not as a state attorney's aide. Maybe he moonlights."

"She. Adelaide Farndon."

"Makes it on the fringe benefits. Sells a little ass. Frugal with the housekeeping money."

CD laughed, said the whole world had gone to hell, and went to his laptop to find out what he could about Adelaide Farndon. It seems she was from an independently wealthy family living part time in Miami and part time in Mexico City and part time in Cali, Colombia. She handled appointments and assignments and court dates. She selected which judge would handle which case. Things like that.

Well, DUH! I can't see anything wrong there!

CD Grimes was a state marshal for years. He still held the papers. He would arrange something. It would not be handled by locals. It was Saturday night. A very likely time for something to be going down.

CD's boat, the Nicely Done Too, came up the channel and stayed just outside the fancy yacht at the dock. There were a dozen or so teenage boys and girls on the deck of the Dare2Bea, dancing to a small live band and drinking beer and booze supplied on a decktop bar.

Two carloads of special police stopped in front and went to the door, where they were denied entrance by a couple of overmuscled hoods. They shoved the hoods aside, two cops patted them down and put them in handcuffs. They went in.

Four of the police went onto the deck and waved to CD, who came alongside and boarded.

A rather fiery attractive woman came rushing from the master cabin to demand what was going on.

"It's called a raid," CD answered. "It seems there are a few underage citizens imbibing in strong alcoholic beverages supplied by a bar on the deck."

A cop came to whisper to him. He said to arrest everyone on the boat and in the house. He turned toward the woman to say, "And marijuana and cocaine are being used by those same minors, which means I seize all properties associated with the illegalities as state marshal. I advise that you say nothing without benefit of counsel. Anything you say will be held against you in a court of law.

"Sgt. Adams, I think you will have to call for two or three more paddy wagons, huh?"

"At least!"

"Look! We can explain this! I want to talk to you in private!" the woman cried. "I have to make a couple of calls. This will all blow over in ten minutes, I promise!"

"You can make one call after processing," Adams said. "Let's go!"

"You could end up cut crab bait, shithead!" she snarled. "You wouldn't be the first!"

"She just admitted to murder!" CD cried, aping shock.

"Fuck you! You don't know who you're going up against!"

"He's CD Grimes. You're A. Farndon. No lawyer in this state and fifty nine others doesn't know who CD Grimes is! You think you're going to scare him, think again! He can buy and sell your whole cartel ten times over, and he's clean," Adams said, conversationally.

"ER! CD, er, what ... oh, shit!"

"That about covers it. Let's go."

Adams slapped the cuffs on her and started toward the dock, almost dragging her. She was very colorful in her choice of vulgar obscenities. CD said he'd go to the station to make out the affidavit he would see was followed exactly.

He went home, called Fred, checked that the jet was loaded properly and went to bed.

Tomorrow, paradise!

CD and Alma were staying in a cabin just a little down the beach from Clint and Tyna that Clint and Nito had constructed for a guest house. Nick and Janet would arrive later. CD and Clint would go to Chiriqui Grande to meet Nick and Janet. CD would meet with the crew who were going to build the houses on the island. They were to start construction today. The early crew were coming into the beach when Clint and CD headed for Chiriqui Grande. Alma and Tyna were in Clint's smaller boat on the way to the island.

It was a little drizzly at Chiriqui Grande, but was the kind of misty rain the people there ignored. After all, this was a coastal rain forest area!

CD went to the office of the aduana where the building crew were waiting while the government people checked out the supplies that had been imported.

None. That went fast! They were headed for the island less than fifteen minutes later. Clint would wait for Nick and Janet at the bombas. He had his car to take whatever they brought to the boat.

Rojelio came to say Clint might be interested to know that two men and a woman had been asking a lot of strange questions about the Campbells. He refused them any information, saying it was an on-going investigation. They made some statements intended to scare him into believing some bigshots from Panamá City would come and put him in his own cell if he didn't 'cooperate.'

"I was all innocence. I asked if they were threatening a police officer. They said they were warning a police officer. I said there was no legal difference. How would the lot of them like to spend ninety days in carcel?"

"To which they replied?"

"They just left."

"If they come back, or if anyone else asks too many questions or if you are threatened again in any way, call me. You have my number. There's something very fishy going on here!"

"Fishing? I don't...?"

"An expression. It means 'very strange' in trans-lation."

"Thank you, Clint. You are a friend. I will call you if there are further things to happen. I will certainly investigate the Campbell people as best I can."

"Take care, my friend."

"I will. Very certainly."

Clint soon went on to the bombas. He was there for twenty minutes or so, talking with a number of people he knew. A busload of people on their way to Isla Colón stopped for snacks and the rest rooms. Clint told them about some of the places that would appeal to the different ages and interests.

The next bus was the one Janet and Nick were on. They loaded all their stuff into Clint's car, drove to the dock to transfer it into the boat, Clint took the car back to the friend's place where he kept it (the friend used it a lot. Clint, almost never anymore.). They headed for Cusapín. Clint pointed to an island on the horizon and said that was it.

"Do you mean that mountain?" Janet asked. "I had pictured a quaint little island with a lot of coconut palm trees, like our place on Martinique!"

"It has plenty of that," Clint replied. "It also has bananas and pineapples and cashews and almonds and guanabana and oranges and lemons and avocados and mangos and mormones and jobitos and papayas and fifty others. Alma is going crazy. There are hundreds of varieties of orchids there. She found four types of vanilla already, some with seed capsules ready to make vanilla flavoring. You saw from before how the real thing is a thousand times as flavorful as the crap in the states. We have fish and other seafoods of almost any type as well as plenty of the natural food vegetables. I'll plant any that aren't already there. I think you could eat very well for six months and never have the same things twice in the time."

"We were here for two weeks before. We didn't have the same meal twice then, except when we were in David eating in the fancy restaurants. I like the native foods, except that every meal has to have rice, which I ain't that fond of," Nick said. "In the restaurants I could usually have potatoes, instead. I had to get used to not having bread with most meals.

"I did learn there were a lot of rice dishes that were good. Coconut rice is delicious. That rice pudding Alma made with coconut, pineapple and raisins was fantastic, but she's got to be the best cook in the world! I like curry dishes with rice."

"You should have known Ben and Earl, on Isla Colón," Tyna said. She had just come from the house where she had opened the guest room and readied it for them. "Earl was a cordon bleu chef and Ben was a natural cook. Together ... well!

"I have some local things in the freezer. Conch, fish, crab, lobster, chicken, iguana, pork. You can fix whatever you like. We have to eat all that stuff before we move to the island. Clint will take the solar panels and storage, so we'll have everything about the same as here. Our one import from so-called civilized society. Electric stuff. There's TV and DVD and all that. We almost never use it. Clint uses the comp sometimes. He's mostly retired from the detective thing. Only when it affects the comarca and our people or when it's something he can't resist. He's a born detective. It's like that thing in one of Dave's books about a yak."

"I think I remember that. I read a lot of his books. Nick read a few of them," Janet said. "I liked that one. A Japanese man, talking about some of the people he was forced to do business with. 'You can take a yak from the fields, have it hand curried and petted by twelve beautiful virgins, feed it only the selected finest of grains, put it in a golden corral with the softest fine straw. It will remain a yak.' Something like that."

"I say you can take the animal out of the barn, but you can't take the barn out of the animal," Nick said. "If you're raised in a barn, you'll bray like a barn animal. Trite, but very true. It's all in how you was raised. Parents are pigs, you'll be a pig. In the work, I always admired anyone who could beat that rut. A few did. I saw several bigtime gangsters turn legitimate. I admired them for the strength it took to do that."

"Yeah. Greco and Donilleti. Mo Jefferson. I've heard of them. I had a friend who was as big (Marko Bocinni, who lived in Bocas as Manny Mathews. He raised a family he could be proud of), who turned one eighty. Pillar of the community. Pancho knows him. He calls Pancho Pancho (Anyone who called Pancho by his nickname, not "Mr. DeGulio, Sir!" was a close friend).

They talked for a long time. Janet and Nick moved in. Tyna and Janet were doing some things around the house, Nick and Clint went to the little village for Nick's friends there to welcome him to the comarca.

It would be like that for about a month, then the island.

*

Nick and Janet met Clint at the bus stop and went to his place on the comarca in his boat. They moved into the guest room. The wives were doing something, getting ready to move to the island. He and Clint went to the village, where he remade his contacts with many of those fantastic people.

He could fit here. That had worried him. CD and Clint were millionaires – billionaires, in CD's case – but both preferred the lifestyle of the comarca.

He didn't think he could adjust to not having anything to do. Clint and CD were the same. Janet and Alma and Tyna were the same. He fully intended to become part of the comarca. He liked the responsible but easy lifestyle. He hoped he could become half as close to the Indios as Clint. He would have to get used to hugs whenever they met somewhere else or after he had been away for any length of time. They were a touching people.

They returned to the house after a couple of hours. CD was on the island. They would go out. Jan and Tyna would go over tomorrow. Alma was hands-on about the construction, but not the bossy type. She would pitch in and help. Jan was like that.

Clint had some work to do around the place. He said it was small things that needed doing. Nick could do what he wanted.

Nick went to the beach to walk along. Two small boys and a girl came to walk with him. They didn't speak English, his Spanish was poor. He knew "Jantoro!" in the dialect meant welcome or good or something positive. It was a greeting as used by the Guayme, the neighboring Indios. "Coin" meant the same thing and was used more by the Ngobe, though both used both terms.

These kids were seven or eight years old and were a kilometer away from home on a beach, alone. They were safer that any kids that age almost anywhere in the states. They knew more about life at that age than most in the USA at fifteen years. They lived with nature. They didn't fight it and didn't try to deny they were human.

The first time he and Janet were there, Nito, Clint's son, was telling about an older boy who had screwed him. Clint and Tyna were interested, he and Janet were shocked. Nito just said he didn't much care for it, but it wasn't so bad, either.

Clint saw how he was reacting and said it happened to most people. Big deal! Why try to make the kid think he'd done anything wrong? Nito had consented. If he'd been raped, it would be a different thing. That, you take out on the one who did the raping, not on the victim.

He agreed, intellectually. Emotionally was a different thing.

Nito wasn't harmed by it in any way. He was as well-adjusted as most of the Indio kids and was making a name for himself in police circles. Clint's daughter was making as much of a name for herself in medical.

He'd been back twice since that first trip. He saw that this society worked in ways the so-called "civilized" failed

He chatted happily with the kids. They seemed to understand what he meant, even if they didn't know the words. He understood them. They did pick up a few English words. He learned that "dere" meant afternoon. When they parted, he said, "Jantoro dere!" They laughed and replied, "Coin dere!" The girl simply said, "Co!" He thought that was a shortened form of "Coin" they used as a reply.

He went to the house. Janet and Tyna were cooking a large spiny langosta for dinner. CD was back. Clint would be back when he got back. Nobody had a schedule.

He found he was sunburned. He'd forgotten he had been inside so much and walked for more than two hours on a beach in the full sunlight!

Tyna used some aloe that was right by the door and had him eat four large carambolas. They are a very high quality source of vitamin C. The inflamation was gone in half an hour or so, and the soreness. He had a little tan from Florida, so it wasn't a severe burn. In the morning it was hardly noticeable.

Things went along like that for the next two days, then Clint said he had a case he was going to spend some time on. He had retired more than thirty times before, but something that intrigued him came along now and then.

"Two people were killed. Their car was pushed over the side of a mountain with them in it. I solved that in a day, but those two didn't exist a couple of years ago. Now some strange people are asking a lot of questions. I want to know what's behind it."

"When I came on that kind of thing it almost always turned out to be someone on witness protection."

"I have someone who can usually check that kind of thing fast. I don't think so."

"I can check with Pancho. He finds that kind of thing faster than anyone else I've encountered."

"I did. He can't find anything.

"Want a little diversion?"

"It could be interesting."

Clint used the computer to contact Manny Mathews, who was actually a retired mafia don from California Clint had helped to establish a new identity. He went legitimate, but had held onto his power. He couldn't find much. The Campbells could be Larry Holden and Marsha Peabody. They had disappeared at about the same time two years ago. They had some kind of information the US military wanted or didn't want out or something such. The only connection he could find between them was e-mails that seemed to be coded, but even that wasn't certain.

Clint thought. JK, who worked for CD for years, was a genius when it came to computers. He had developed a number of programs that decoded whatever needed decoding. He was on his own island in the Caribbean. Clint could call him, but it might be better if CD did.

He called to the island. CD used his special cellular phone with the coded and scrambled signal. JK would check and call back when he had anything. Send him a number.

JK could find almost anything about almost anyone if he had any kind of number that would be somewhere on the net. A Social Security or passport number was best, but even an old address or phone number could be traced easily. A drivers' license or fishing license, a license tag number – so long as it was a number that anyone would have registered for any reason with any government agency.

Clint had the passport numbers, but said they led to people who didn't exist a couple of years ago.

That wouldn't slow JK for one second! CD also gave him the names, Larry Holden and Marsha Peabody and the information, uncertain, that they had something the military was interested in, though what that was about was a thing they could only guess at at this point.

Nick strolled in with Janet. She said "Hi!" and went back toward their cabin. She was going with Alma and Tyna to Cusapín to help set up the materials for the new school year. Clint explained the case. Nick said he would like to try his hand at it. He knew from his trips before that the law was handled differently here than in Florida.

"We can each use our own methods. We share anything we learn. This isn't some kind of competition unless or until something comes up that lets us have some fun with it," Clint suggested. "We did have that one time we all worked on a case. It took us each the same time to solve it." (*Murder Divided by 3*)

"I'll use the secure comp in my plane with JK first. He's the best bet we have to find who the Campbells were," CD decided. "If something military is involved, Crane's security clearances, particularly JK's, are for the top of the top secret crap."

"JK was a big help to us a few years ago when that FBI man was murdered. That tied it to the Russian mafia. I was very damned glad Pancho is a friend there!" (Nick Storie book 16: *Bad Move*)

"I think I can trace backward from something on a note to find who hired the killings," Clint said. "That will tell us if the military is behind it. I don't want the US military doing anything here in Panamá. They would work through the CIA, and that leads inevitably to disaster."

For the time being, Nick would stay on the comarca, CD would go to David, where his jet was hangared, Clint would go to Isla Colón.

*

Nick walked along the beach in thought. He went to the computer and started bringing up past records of Larry Holden. All he knew about him from the information Clint supplied was that he was from Fresno, California, had worked for various companies having to do with home security. He had invented an infra-red movement detector that was popular. He was fairly wealthy from royalties.

The military had those things out the ying-yang. There had to be more.

He went to the patent description. From what little he knew, Nick thought it was a standard type of thing.

He traced the name through the patent offices. Holden had also patented a very small laser range finder. It had applications for construction. It was accurate to within four inches at one mile.

That could very well have military significance!

Okay. Just for a direction, he would concentrate on that.

Why would the military have him assassinated for that? It was patented. Anyone could get the manufacturing specs and build the thing, so long as Holden got royalties. Snipers and missiles and what have you could use it – so long as they considered other factors. A thirty mile an hour cross-wind would make the accuracy within four feet instead of four inches. Drop or rise, another consideration.

Page 87

Also, Holden's invention would put him in it, not the woman. What was her connection?

Marsha Peabody. Born in Oregon, worked in Silicon Valley for a few years. Patented a laser-driven self-focusing microscope. A boon to electron microscopes that had a problem when the focus was off at one millionth of an inch. Her ultra-short focusing laser held focus at three ten-millionths of an inch.

That was all.

Would combining those two things give any better view ... no. Millionths of an inch had no application at a mile.

There had to be something. Nick was sure he had a part of an answer. Too bad he didn't really know what the question was!

**

Clint asked around. It was too bad he didn't have Judi Lum here to help him. There had been no one in the world more able in getting information.

From what he knew and suspected, his quarry would go to the Toro Loco and the Rip Tide. He or she would be the slightly obnoxious pushy type.

Santo Smith, an Indio friend, said it could be the Warren woman. Kind of brassy, but fun. From Texas. She went to the Toro Loco and to Gary's.

"She's easy to find. You're a gringo, so she'll call you Fred. I'm Indio, so she calls me Tonto. She calls the Latins Pedro and the blacks Sambo."

Anderson was black – but she might have assumed he was Latino.

At seven thirty Clint went into the Toro Loco. He spotted Margarita Warren right away. She was at the bar, ordering drinks for everyone. There were six others beside Clint and her in the place. She announced she had bought all the guys a drink. That meant she was entitled to get in their pants. Isn't that the way men thought?

"You don't have to buy me a drink for that! I'm ready without it!" one man said quickly.

"And if I didn't get there first, you would have bought me a drink and figured you owned me for the night, right?" It was obviously a routine with her. The guys seemed to like her. This was a standing joke.

She noticed Clint. "New face! First dibs!" she cried.

"No problem. The gay guys aren't here until later," another fired back.

"You don't prefer gay guys, do you? With my luck, you would."

Clint fell right into the joke. "Only on alternate Thursdays. This is Friday."

"You look like a gringo, but not like a gringo. What?"

"Ngobe. Call me Tonto."

Santo came in just before that. He said, "No! I'm Tonto! She can call you abuelo!"

She laughed. "I'm Rita. You are?"

"Clint. I'll call you Sally."

"Sally? If there's one thing I'm not, it's a Sally. You that famous dick?"

"He's the famous dick. Both kinds," Santo replied.

"She said dick. Not dickhead," John, a man Clint knew for years, said. Clint gave him the bird.

They had a good time, joking most of the three hours Clint spent there. She got him aside one time for a few minutes and asked if he was looking for her.

"No more. I found you. Same process with you as with Anderson or do you know who you're working for?"

"Cool! What gave me away?"

"Pedro. Aces."

She nodded and grinned. "I don't know what it's about. I get a free vacation in heaven for it. Politics in it, but they were spies from Iran. They swore that."

"They were Americans from California and Oregon who had some information about some politicians."

She looked shocked. "You aren't shitting me, are you?"

"No."

"If I knew, I think I'd tell you. I'll damned well find out!"

"No! You'd be a spy they would hire someone else to get rid of! Just don't let anyone know you or I said anything except that this is a really open society where you can have fun. I'll handle it my own way."

"They really would. Deal, Sam Spade!"

The rest of the night went well. Clint had a few things he wanted to do in the morning, then would head back home.

***

"JK, I have to get some information on a couple of people who didn't exist two years ago. Military might be involved. Not WP." CD gave him what information he had. JK would get back.

CD had a lot of experience with the military. Crane manufactured various top secret devices. He wasn't able to get out of that end because of the past. Crane had been used through a lot of things, each of less worth than the last. It was sickening to know what governments had become. Greedy little people vying for money and position, then didn't know what to do with it when they had it. So they went after more.

He was glad to be away from that. His kids had it to deal with. He was sorry he couldn't divest and tell the whole world to kiss his ass.

JK sent the information as he found it. Nothing new. Both he and JK felt that knowing the connection with the two people would probably give them the answers they were after. JK would trace back further. Maybe he could find where the two met. That could be the basis for what happened since that time.

CD got his helicopter and went to the island. The house would be ready for occupancy in another week. Alma was already designing and building her orchid jungle. JK called to say he'd sent what might mean a lot. It was from before either of them invented anything. It would be in scrambled code at the jet. He even told CD that in a code they had worked out. It sounded like he was asking about the construction of the house.

CD got back to the chopper and headed for David.

The code light was on. That was a sign that JK's little invention that found listeners had found listeners. What they wouldn't know was that the two of them would chat about things at the Crane plant while a totally separate system downloaded what they were really finding.

Just to be mean, CD discussed a top secret laser device they were developing for the space program, such as it was at the moment. He was sure no one listening had authorization to hear a word of it. The real part was in a special code it would take eight months to decipher, if they could find the base at all. When it was all there, JK said he had a project he was studying to make light turn back on itself.

The governments who knew of JK would go crazy trying to figure how that could be done. They knew that, if JK Kiley said it would work, it would work.

The coded way he said it was that you did that every time you looked in a mirror, but the "DUH!-geniuses" in the military would never think of something so obvious. Maybe ten million of their budget would go to try to find a way to turn light back on itself.

CD giggled and went to the downloaded files. They seemed to be videos.

First was Marsha Peabody behind a podium. CD listened as she expounded on inserting a reader in a focusing unit that used a Dopler effect program to give an exact distance as close as a ten millionths of an inch at one inch or one half inch at one mile.

It seemed there was a way ... maybe that was the principle of Holden's invention.

There were short flashes of two other people giving speeches, then Holden. This was where they first met. This was where two ideas combined to ... what?

He watched three more videos, only one of which Holden appeared in.

It seemed to be extensions of what the first had been. She had come up with a device that used the Dopler effect to find things that ... so that was it! A combination of Holden's device and hers would make it possible, even probable, that you could hit a target within half an inch of dead center at three miles distance!

Was that a military motive or not? Dead-accurate snipers at three miles was getting pretty well up there.

Why would they kill the two inventors? What was he missing?

Nick sat back to think. He had found a thing or two. The two dead people had made speeches at the same seminaries. All that was public property. Shutting them up made no difference to anything he could see.

He called Clint to discuss what was known so far. Clint conferenced CD into it. CD and he were doing the "what?" part while Clint did the "who?" part. It seemed that Holden and Peabody had come up with a device that could have pinpoint accuracy at three miles and that, seeing how screwed up it already seemed, the CIA was likely to be behind the assassinations. After the chat Nick went back to the computer, but couldn't think of anything to check. It would be tangental. JK would probably be the one to find anything.

Maybe.

Why were they in Panamá? Was it just a coincidence – or were they here for a specific reason?

Another thing to think about. Did they communicate ... they would have had to. They communicated in a way that someone was able to tap into. That they had invented something was a likely scenario.

He used the special phone JK had given him several years ago that he used about four times per year to keep up to date with him. JK said he had fiddled with the idea a bit. Maybe he could find a tidbit or two. He had the e-mails and blogs the two had used. Some kind of rough system was used to scramble a lot of it up, but that kind of thing was patterned. He could get around most of it.

They chatted about the island. JK would like to visit.

When they rang off Nick sat back to think. A few minutes later JK started sending him the e-mails he could use.

He had another idea and asked that JK send a list of all e-mail addresses either received or sent to. He had several hundred addresses and correlated them.

He felt he had something useful in that, but couldn't think of what.

He scrolled down the lists on split screen. Both sent things to two addresses that never responded in any way.

What was that about? If they sent something to an address a couple of times and got no response they would probably not send anything else.

He saw the spiral arrow on every one of those messages. He was about to ask JK what it meant, then remembered seeing the arrows on his own e-mail. It meant the message was forwarded to that address.

He checked the sources of the forwarded messages. They were all scientific research papers.

He called JK. He asked if it was possible the addresses were storage areas. JK started to ask what he was talking about, but said, "So. They each have a site they use to store and study the newest ideas and theories. They didn't directly communicate through their regular e-mails, but I'll bet those two sites communicated!"

"Would the CIA or whatever figure that out?"

"Huh! Only if somebody drew them a diagram! I'll see what I can find at those two addresses. I'll get back to you. Is CD in on it?"

"Yeah, JK. Him and Clint."

Rita Warren was out of it past being the block point if anyone came this far. That meant concentrating on the three people who had tried to intimidate Rojelio. This was a disconnected mess. Nick or CD might come up with something to form at least a basic link.

Clint went back to Chiriqui Grande to talk with Rojelio. He got the information collected. Rojelio had the sense to get his information in ways they wouldn't know. Nito had shown him how to check for passport numbers and such at hotels and for use of credit cards and license numbers, among others.

Irene Mary Smith from Baltimore, Maryland. Tourist. Used Master Card in name of Jefferson Lincoln Company through KFSC Diversified, Orlando, Florida. He couldn't find much about the company. Small manufacturer of specialized application connectors. What the hell did that mean?

She was a fashion designer.

Thomas Allen Jones, Houston, Texas. Tourist. Used Visa Card in name of StartlersStarters, Inc. A small company that produced starters for fluorescent lights. He was a carpenter.

Robert William Brothers, Atlanta, Georgia. Tourist. Used Visa Card in name of Jefferson Applicators. Another small company that didn't seem to do anything. He was a used car salesman.

Let's see. Three people with common names who used credit cards from companies they didn't work for. That smelled strongly of CIA. A fashion designer, a carpenter and a used car salesman acting like big bad govmint agents y'all asking about murdered inventors of things with military applications.

KFSC. Kentucky Fried Space Chicken?

He checked the company. There was a little less than nothing about it available. A Dr. Alexander Fieldinghouse was, apparently, chairman and CEO.

He checked on Fieldinghouse. He was a specialist in mineral deprivation on the cellular level for NASA.

He might well work with electron microscopes, but so what?

Nothing even that interesting in the others.

Either there was a connection with NASA – no! It was set up to make people who investigated think that! If there was one sure thing, this wasn't directly linked to NASA. If it was there would be no such item to catch the eye. It was too far for it to be CIA. This was all crap that was designed to keep anyone from finding anything.

Okay. Something that would strike within a half inch in three miles of very difficult trajectory. A sniper's tool.

What about at a hundred miles?

He sat back to study some papers, but there didn't seem to be that much more. He was still at square one.

He decided to see if he could accidentally run into the three. Rojelio said they were staying at the hotel last night. They had gone somewhere in the morning and would be back in the late afternoon, according to Luis, at the hotel desk.

Clint went into the restaurant to sit at a table next to three gringos to order the carne corriente. The three seemed very interested in him, so he smiled and asked if he had done anything to draw attention to himself. Irene answered, "Aren't you Clint Faraday?"

"So I'm told."

"You were a close friend of that Dave character who invented some kind of super weapon the Indios used?"

"Dave? Yes."

"Did you ever see the weapon?"

"They tell me I did. I didn't know that's what it was. I can't tell you anything about it except it looks like something very ordinary." (Clint Faraday book 19: *A Moving Target*)

"We went to Cusapín. We talked with your wife. She said she'd heard about it, but didn't have time for such things. Those two gringas with her said they knew Dave from Florida, but didn't know anything about any super weapon. One is ... I guess you would know. They were at the place Grimes is building. Grimes owns Crane, who produce weapons for the US military."

"Alma? Janet and Tyna. None of them interfere with the husbands' work. They're individuals with their own interests, one of which is definitely *not* weapons. Dave was more about the orchids with them."

"I'm Bob Brothers. The Indios shot down planes at three kilometers? How could they get such an accurate aim? I hear the holes they had in them were the size of a nickel!"

"I really don't know. Dave explained once to that Leventhal person. I heard it. It was about time and a velocity of sixty or seventy thousand miles per hour, so there weren't any detectable, what did he say? Perturbations? Something about time ... something. Dilatation in a contained volume? Something."

Clint would have a little fun here. He did know a little about the weapon. Dave used some arguments about it that he said were pure bullshit, but the donkey/carrot military scientists would fall for it.

"Gheee? Seventy thousand miles per hour? That would vaporize whatever he was shooting!" the one Clint assumed was Tom Jones cried.

"Marbles. He said that wouldn't matter because it would be halfway to the moon before any of the molecules had time to separate or something. Once out of the atmosphere it would all coalesce."

"Marbles? What...?" Irene asked.

"He once picked up a child's marble on the road and said it was hard to believe a ten year old could build something with things found in a garbage dump that would shoot an object like that through the hardest armor we made. It could shoot down the stealth bomber. It was silent. I don't remember much. It wasn't something I could get interested in unless it was used as a murder weapon. Military? Who gives a happy shit?"

"But ... how does it work?"

"I don't have a clue. Something about eddy currents and vibrations and time distortion."

"A glass marble? You can't produce eddy currents in glass!" Jones cried.

"No, I can't. He could, I suppose. The thing did work.

"Ah, here's my repast. Excuse me. Have a good evening."

The rest of the time he was there the three were arguing about marbles and glass and eddy currents. They wanted to ask Clint what he meant about time, but it was too plain he didn't want to be disturbed while he ate. When he finished, he stood, nodded at them and walked out before they could question him again.

He went to the boat and contacted CD and Nick to tell him the latest. It was about aiming Dave's weapon.

"But they don't have any such weapon," CD pointed out. "JK talked about it with Dave. He says it's what Dave claimed, so far as he could discover. It would as much as destroy civilization if it got out. A ten year old could build it and it would shoot down the stealth bomber – and more. If you knew any nutcase or terrorist or whatever could build one and shoot you down, would you get on a plane?"

"Sort of the same he told us. One person could cut off a highway or hole a gas line or generator or whatever. It works because of something in his theory of the omniverse.

"If JK says it works, it's sort of scary."

"I've heard you like understatement."

They chatted a minute, then rang off. Was this a case of some organization adding one and one and getting seven point five four? Was even the CIA that stupid?

To Clint, it looked a bit too much for CIA. They weren't involved. They fucked up things after they got into them and while getting into them. This was making it seem like the idiot phase was before. *Not* their style.

***

CD took the laptop from the chopper into the cabin and put it onto the table in the kitchen. He took the BugChaser from the bag of groceries (it was disguised as a gas sparker/starter) and glanced at the tell-tale as he laid it on the stove. There was an electronic device in the room.

He put a pan of water on the stove and used the starter to ignite the gas. It didn't take the first flick. He flicked it again.

Page 99

The device was under the edge of the shelf. He laid the sparker almost on top of it and called to ask if Alma was close. He knew she was at the island. Calling made the BugChaser note that the bug was video and audio. One circuit sound-accessed, the other motion accessed.

He put a spoonful of instant coffee in a cup and poured the hot water over it (which should be a dead giveaway if they knew anything at all about him. He drank only the special mix of coffee Alma made). He added a spoon of sugar, then sat at the table to take his cell phone out of its case and make a call (that was to a recorder on his jet). The call would go out scrambled and coded. They would feel they had what they needed from what he said.

He acted like he was making a report to JK. He said he had determined that the people in question were operatives, but not from NASA, FBI, CIA or Pentagon. That meant they were agents for someone else. The last thing the US, even the military, wanted was for the inventors of such a thing killed. It was low possibility that there could be any defense against the item in focus, but they would be that low possibility. Only JK, in his experience with such things – and he had a *lot* of experience through Crane – could possibly find a defense.

Who would want ... he stopped. Who, indeed?

He sent the code for JK to actually read what he was sending. He might have stumbled on something.

The light came on that said JK was listening.

"JK, someone has been threatened with that weapon. It's stronger than when Dave said he would put instructions on the web and other places if certain practices weren't stopped."

"It's likely. Dave made his threat against corrupt politicians, but the big money people got the message. If such a thing were to be released, they know damned well they would be the first targets. The world's become a slavehold for those people and everyone knows it. It's why you're smart to be on that comarca. The crumble of the money world won't affect the Indios. I can't see ... I'll be damned. So that's what it is! It's everything Dave said it was. It's something the militaries of every advanced country on Earth have be doing research on. He found a way to make it work! I'll be damned!"

"What?"

"I know what Dave's weapon is. I'll make one this afternoon to test. It really is something simple beyond your ability to believe. This is rich!"

He caught himself. He realized CD wouldn't be doing this for any reason except to throw off listeners. He might have said too much, but he would try to fix that. He remembered how Clint reported that he snowed them with BS.

"CD, every country on this planet has been working on a laser-driven fusion reactor. We've all had a little success. It's a matter of a *sustained* reactor. Dave's zero theory says that only time and motion exist. He propounded on that fact hundreds of times. That's what the gyroscope experiments were about.

"I'll be dog-damned! He was right about wrapping yourself in a different time volume. It's so damned easy to do, particularly when your volume is less than a cubic foot."

CD caught on. This babble had nothing to do with the weapon, it was to get them looking in all the wrong places.

"I follow a little. Explain."

"A gyroscope affects time along Einsteinian lines. The omniverse is time and motion in fixed equation. Increase one and you increase the other to the exact same balance, but mirror. Increase time, decrease motion. Decrease motion, increase time.

"The thing simply emplaces an eddy in time in any object whatever. It increases time. You place the object in that frame and move it in a direction, always a straight line by inertial laws. You increase motion within that frame, then revert instantly back to what we consider normal. The object increases its motion directly in this frame as time drops to the same ratio. C squared, remember, so you get a logarythmic function on the base determiner.

"What happens, you move an object at fifty miles per hour in a time frame a reverse multiple of what we call 'here' in this frame. Suddenly remove the barrier, so to speak. The object is suddenly moving at the multiple in this frame. It's Einsteinian and in balance. The object you were moving at fifty miles per hour in that frame is now moving at a hundred thousand miles per hour in this frame. Not that much. Cubed ... scale fourth log ... eighty seven thousand miles per hour. Whatever. I have an idea."

JK was known to get an idea and simply walk away like the rest of the world didn't exist. CD knew this was to scare the holy living piss out of whoever was behind this mess. It was pure crap from the get-go. They would definitely know JK was a genius without equal. They'd probably work for hours to find what a logarythmic function on a base determiner was.

Now. See what fish strikes at that lure!

Nick and friends were looking over the house on the island. It was going faster than CD or Nick could believe. They expected delays and additions and permits and bureaucracy. Clint knew he was respected by what few such agencies had involvement. The Indios building the house would work on this as if it were Clint working with them on a project for the comarca. Nick and CD and wives were getting used to the hugs every time they met any of the people from the comarca. The kids were working as much as their fathers. The younger ones doing the lighter work. Two of the girls, maybe eight or nine years old, were keeping food available. They were already good cooks.

The boys between six and ten were making the garden plots or working on Alma's orchid gardens.

It was near noon, so everyone stripped and went into the river that ran a few hundred meters from the house to cool off and clean up. Nick, Janet, CD and Alma seemed uncertain, then stripped and joined them. The men wrestled and dunked each other. They played and laughed a lot.

Clint saw Janet sitting on a large flat rock, crying. He asked why.

"This is beautiful."

"What?"

"Life. All of it."

He nodded. They all climbed onto the rocks to sit for a few minutes to dry off, put on their clothes, and went to the meal. This one was a sort of seafood stew. It was a little like paella. Muscles, lobster, crab, fish, conch, shrimp, octopus in a brown sauce served over rice. It had a slightly curry flavor. There was a pasta salad with pineapple, banana, coconut and flakes of jobito with a dressing not unlike mayonaise. Guanabana chicha and/or coffee.

"My God!" Janet exclaimed. "I've eaten in the best restaurants! These kids could put them out of business in a week!

"Oh, Nick! When we were married you promised me the stars and planets! This is so much more!

"Clint, what is this?"

She was holding up a small piece of fruit from the salad.

"Jobito. Smell it."

She did. "Sort of like ... fruit punch?"

"And it tastes like fruit punch."

After the meal Nick, CD, and Clint helped carry the heavy nispero for the house. It is a wood that is as heavy as steel and about as strong. Clint had bought corundum drills for the construction. A regular nail, unless the wood was drilled, would just bend. Concrete nails would penetrate, but would tend to split the wood. It did not deteriorate. It was too hard for termites or bacteria or fungus to affect.

Alma said the red wood was beautiful. She would like to carve some things in it, but didn't have good enough tools. Janet had some tools she used to carve jade. They would both make things.

They went back to Cusapín late in the afternoon. Renaldo said there were three people who had come before and a fourth. They were at the hospidaje. Did Clint want to talk with them or wait until tomorrow?

"I'm off duty today. Tomorrow."

They went to his house. CD got Nick and Clint aside and told them about the bugs. Nick shook his head and looked a little irritated. Clint said he knew. He was going to warn them. He had his own recorders on since this case started. They told about what they had learned and about JK's involvement.

"I can picture their scientists sitting around roaring at each other about logarythmic functions and eddy currents!" Nick said.

"When I said about seventy thousand miles per hour, that Bob Bill Brothers character pissed in his pants," Clint said. "I told JK about that. It's where he came up with his figure.

"I still want to know what it's about. They can kill each other off or whatever. I don't care.

"I don't want them on the comarca. I won't put up with them dragging anyone else into it."

"I want to know who's behind it," Nick replied. "They already had two people killed. We have to get it through to them that was a mistake that never should have been made."

"We have to find why they were killed. None of this will make any sense until we know that."

"Why they were here is more important, I think," Clint warned. "Dave's dead and gone. There's nothing he left that they could be after unless they think he left one of us or one of the Indios with something.

"He did, but not this end of the comarca."

"Maybe that's it. Maybe they only know the thing was used on the comarca and that he spent so much time here," Nick suggested. "I would think we could distract them to another part of the comarca where there isn't anything to grab some time to find who's behind it."

Clint grinned. "Buabidi and Soloy. The museum. We might just accidentally let it slip that Dave said he had put something in the museum archives to be found when directed or when something specific happened.

"Let's go back to the house. I'm tired. Tomorrow might be a fun day, but be careful. Try to get it away from here. The women aren't any least part of it. Get them involved and I'll eliminate them as a problem, myself. Permanently."

They agreed with that.

**

The morning was spectacular. Sunrises are as colorful as sunsets here. The women were going to help in the puebla for awhile, then go to the island. Nick would hitch a ride with CD on the chopper to David. He would check on some ideas there and buy some more practical clothes. What he had was okay in town, but not where he would spend most of his time. CD had to make some arrangements about things in Florida. Clint would do some things around the place and get ready to move to the island. They would all be back by nightfall or would call if they wouldn't get back until tomorrow.

Tomorrow, Clint would go to Buabidi, then return through Soloy. He had innocently made a remark about Dave leaving something at the museum he wanted to study to Tyna last night while standing two feet from one of their bugs.

There was a three day long waiting list for anyone to get into the museum. Clint was Ngobe. The Ngobe could go in anytime they liked. After all, it was *their* museum! (Clint Faraday, book 51: *Dead Man Talking*)

Everyone left except Clint. He went through a lot of things and was setting up the water line to the shower at the palmfrond hut by the beach when four people came strolling casually along. It was Irene and friends and another man. They waved and called and came over. The third man was introduced as Gordon Jones, a friend who just *happened* to be spending a month on Isla Colón and had run into them in Chiriqui Grande.

"Uh-huh. Too much like Key West for my tastes. Another tourist trap in the Caribbean. Whoopee!" Clint replied. "Kind of like the comarca? I would think you were more city-attuned."

"It's beautiful here. Peaceful. I still like more the expensive hotel route," Jones said. "I'm spoiled and lazy and know it." He had a sort of strange accent. He was darker than the other three, but not quite the Latino dark.

"Europe? Your accent?" Clint replied.

"I don't have an accent. All of you do," he replied with a laugh. "Belgium."

"I'm the type who thinks a tent is good enough. I'm just getting too old to live like that anymore. Basic house is fine."

"Yes. You are worth several tens of millions of dollars, but prefer a simple life. I can't understand that, but each to his own.

"You met that scientist who had the age treatment thing (Clint Faraday, book 54: *Death From Natural Causes*). Are you using it? I know you are in your late seventies, yet you appear to be perhaps fifty five."

"No way! JK is using it, but just so long as he can be productive. He's fifty something and looks like maybe thirty."

"I heard about that, but don't quite believe it. Is that doctor really a hundred years old?"

"A hundred forty or so. Yes."

"Why didn't this Dave character use it? He was doing a lot of things that needed finishing." He seemed to know immediately he shouldn't have mentioned Dave. He colored. "So. Now you know this isn't a chance encounter."

"Never thought it was."

"It's about that weapon. It has a lot of people almost terrified. The evidence is that it is what he said. If it were to be described it could disrupt modern society somewhat."

"Ah! So you like understatement, too! It would destroy modern society, if what I'm told is true. The very last thing you or anyone else should be doing is trying to find what it is. From what Dave told me, too many people would know what it was if they saw it, but I saw it and didn't know it.

"It wouldn't affect us here. It would be unbelievable what would happen if it was in the hands of most people. Just the part that no plane would dare to ever leave a runway would put civilization into a tailspin that it might not be able to survive. The fact a few people could cut off the food and water and fuel from the cities is, to use a little understatement, myself, chilling. Add that power could be stopped by a nutcase or two.

"I'd estimate more than half the population of the Earth would be dead within three months. After it starts, the big money people who have used and manipulated the world more and more would all be fertilizer. Not one politician would survive more than a week. Most bureaucrats would be among the late.

"Yet you come here to try to find it? Have you considered that there's no defense?"

"We're looking for what it is so we can develop a defense!"

"Listen closely. This is something Dave and *JK Kiley* said. Concentrate.

"*There is no defense.* You could nuke any area where it was known, but that would be the entire planet."

"It is a device that operates on inertial principles of velocity. There are ways."

"At a few thousand miles per hour, maybe. JK said a little piece of balsa wood traveling at those velocities would penetrate the best armor.

"One other little thing to consider, then we can drop this stupid conversation.

"A bit of nuclear material (he would scare them a bit more with something JK said, as reported by CD) being struck with almost anything at that velocity would compress to critical in a picosecond. Think about it.

"How's the weather in Belgium this time of year?"

"So! That's what was meant by the laser fusion process that, uh, that, um, Dr. Flowers was talking about."

"It's been a bit hot here. Good thing we have the ocean breeze. Not unpleasant at all."

"Point taken. We still have to try."

"Leave the people here out of it. Mess with any of my friends or the comarca and you're crab bait – if you're lucky. Killing the two people who could most likely find some way to help you was stupid beyond belief."

"Which shows you know half of what you think you know. That was done to stop the device being placed into the wrong hands."

"Explain. Maybe I can find a little sympathy for you. They would have to have the device to be able to place it in anyone's hands."

"They had it. They were going to blackmail every government in the world. They wanted to rule the world!"

"What makes you think they had it?"

"They showed pictures of it being used on three plates of one inch armored steel. It penetrated. The scientists said there was no expansion. It had to be what they said."

"Show me the pictures. Also, show me any kind of proof of the penetration thing."

"Come with me to the hotel. I'll use the computer there to have my assistant send everything."

"As you know, I have everything you need in the computers. Come on inside."

Jones turned to the other three, who had been just standing there through this. He told them to go to the hotel, then followed Clint inside. Clint turned on the computer.

There had been one demonstration of the thing, and that only to the Indios on the comarca. They had used three plates of armored steel.

Jones brought up a coded website and told the assistant to send all the material in file "dmsdy." It would come in coded, but Jones had a memory stick with the decoding program.

It was soon on the computer. Jones took out a memory stick and plugged it into the USB port. He opened the program, which was the demonstration on the comarca. There was then a video with an older man called Dr. Franken, who inspected the plates shown in the comarca video. He used very exact calipers and instruments, then declared it was as represented.

The weapon was never shown on the comarca videos. Now a shot of who Clint thought might be Peabody holding a thing that looked like something from the X-Files stockroom. Clint giggled.

"What?"

"The video was made on the comarca, except for the last part. How they got it, I have to find out. It's a true video, but nothing they had anything to do with.

"Does that silly thing Peabody's holding look anything at all like something that's common around the house that a ten year old kid could put together in two hours?"

"You mean they were going to try to blackmail the major governments of the world with a bluff?"

"If you say so. It does explain why they were here. They had to go to the comarca and to one of two people to get that video. One or both are going to have to explain something that can't be explained. That ain't so easy to get away with on the comarca.

"Do you realize that this could have caused the information Dave left to be released? That it would bring about exactly the thing you were trying to avoid?"

"So. I can just ... so!

"Mr. Faraday, there will be no further interference here. We wish to avoid, at any cost, what could have happened."

Clint nodded. He left.

Clint called CD. He said he needed a helicopter ride across the comarca. He had most of the answers – if he could believe them. He sort of felt he could.

***

CD went to the jet to spend two hours on the things JK sent. This was the first time in many years JK didn't come up with answers to many things. He said Peabody, in particular, and Holden, to an extent, were egocentrist and introverted at the same time. They were brilliant in a directed way while not having a very firm grip on reality. Peabody was the type who might threaten the wrong people with something. Maybe she thought she could get her hands on Dave's weapon and blackmail the banks for a few billion or something. Holden would follow her.

"It leaves us with the possibility she actually did try to blackmail the wrong person or persons, huh?"

"I sort of think that may be behind it, CD. It's more than a little scary that she might have found the principle behind the thing. It's simple enough. The danger is that it would soon get out and people would find it, or try to. They would tend to study what she and Holden were doing and connect it. There isn't much connection. Only the aiming part. With what it is, that isn't necessary."

"You know what it is?"

"Sure. Dave showed it to me twenty years ago. I made one a little more advanced than his."

"There really is no defense?"

"Not in any practical sense.

"CD, no agency set them up in a WP deal or anything else. They were doing it on their own. Holden knew enough to be able to do it better than the FBI or whatever. That leaves us with those clowns who killed them and what they're trying to accomplish. They represent something or somebody. I can't find who or what.

Page 112

"CD, there's one person in this world I think could get to the bottom of this. Have Nick contact Pancho. I would, but Nick's the one he would trust over almost anybody."

"He already did. Pancho doesn't know what's going on.. Maybe he can be convinced to search out something. I have to agree he's the key to us ever learning much about this."

"Big money's behind it, somehow. I get that from the questions that aren't answered. About when the subject is suddenly changed."

"Dave said all along that the first to go if the thing gets out will be the money manipulators who've held the world in economic slavery for most of recent history. Next would be politicians and bureaucrats, then anyone who had anyone else pissed at them."

"Be glad you're on that comarca. I'm damned glad I'm on this island. The one possible defense is the weapon, itself. You could get me at five miles range, but I could make damned sure no one nor anything got within five miles of here – by using the thing first. I don't see anyone getting on the comarca to attack you, but you have to never forget the entire Caribbean is open for someone to come in a boat. I'm more than five miles from anything on these islands. No routes or anything else. You don't have that protection."

"If it comes to that I can be on the side where I'm building, anyway. They would have to go between this island and the comarca, and I can protect that – with the weapon."

"I'll make a couple and have them ready to deliver if it gets to that point."

CD knew that JK wouldn't take the chance of having CD or anyone else know what the thing was. He was all too familiar with what could be done to get the information from almost anyone.

"It's coming, isn't it, JK?"

"Eventually. We can hope some things will change before that happens."

"You can't know how glad I am that you're who you are."

"And vice versa."

*

Nick sat back to think for a minute.

There was something that made this a far different thing than it appeared. Something had happened that left him with a suspicion that the person or people behind a lot of this were *not* the ones they had been looking at.

He called Pancho. They discussed what was known. Pancho agreed that, if this was something set up or being used by any government or military agency on the Earth, JK would already know all about it. If it was from some mad scientist angle, JK would know. Peabody and Holden were that, but they were dead because whatever they planned had failed.

If it was anything from the underside of the equation, the mobs and dictators and such, Pancho would know. He would know if it was from political intrigues or whatever.

"Nickie, I think we have ... Nickie, let me check something. I will call again in a few minutes. Someone is manipulating all of the above. It could only be one thing. It could be the one thing that makes the above even exist."

"Greed. I know that, but does that tell us ... I see. I'll wait for your call."

"Nickie, I'm going to take my family to JK's place. You and CD convince your own family to come with me. We can try to stop this, but it will be dangerous beyond any of our experiences. CD is among the wealthy, but his pitiful billions are nothing to these people. He was never in their select circle. If he had been, he would be in full control of Crane and would have several trillion dollars, not just a hundred billion. No one would know anything about him. The way it's set up, he would appear to have a couple of million and to live well, but the rest would be hidden.

"Call CD and Clint together. I will call in exactly one hour."

Nick rang off, thought for a minute, then called Clint and CD. They would be on the island in one hour.

Clint and Nick got out of Clint's boat at the little dock down from the house. CD came to greet them and ask what was going on. Nick explained that Pancho would call in about fifteen minutes. He had found who was behind the killings, if not why. He suspected Peabody and Holden were trying to terrorize the banks into giving them a few million dollars or something.

"They were trying to blackmail every government on Earth to become dictators," Clint replied. He explained what he'd learned.

"That fits with what Pancho thinks. Pancho is taking his family to JK's. He wants you two to get your families to go with him. JK has the weapon. He's going to make a couple to get to us if this happens. The one defense from the weapon is the weapon. It will be a local and temporary defense. We can defend here and JK can defend his islands. The comarca won't be much affected, the cities are death traps that very few can escape.

"This is like a horror show, but it's very real."

"A fantasy horror show. We're living in it. If I'm dreaming, please! God that I don't believe in! Wake me up!" Nick cried.

Pancho called. Everything would be in place and ready. He was safe enough for the moment, but they had to be ready. They would have ten minutes to move if it came about.

"... and Clint. You asked, several times, why so many weird things with international importance happened in Panamá. Do you see, now?"

Clint paused. "Yeah, Pancho. Because one or more of those people are right here. The question is, who? Can we root them out and get them out of here?"

"Yes. We must root them out. They are not reptilian or any of that silliness, except in thought patterns. They have made themselves a breed apart. I think their part of evolution is about past.

"You will say we must warn them or something, but I say, 'Why would you want to?'

"I will investigate in my way, with what methods and tools at my disposal. All of you do the same.

"These people have caused wars and worse. Think of them as mass murderers on the order of and worse than Hitler, Pol Pot, and Stalin combined.

"I am serious about this."

They had to agree with that.

*

Nick walked slowly along the beach. This was truly paradise.

Why here? Why now? When everything was falling into place to where he could find some peace and contentment, why did it have to suddenly cave in like this?

He had lived a charmed life and knew it. He had often said he had to be the luckiest one slob in the world.

He was here. It was the place all this crap would affect least. His luck was running on full tilt. The same was true of CD and Clint. CD had always had an easy life in most ways. Clint had started a hard life that had turned into a fantastic one.

All of them took danger to others as a personal affront when it came from the sleazebags of the world. All of them had very strong senses of right and wrong. They agreed on most points. They were also, after life's lessons, pragmatic to a degree they hadn't been in earlier life.

His son and daughter had been convinced to take a month's vacation with Pancho and family on JK's islands. CD's family and Tony Jacobi's family from Florida were going.

It wouldn't be possible to take along a lot of friends. A place where one had to be practical. JK was practical. He said who could or could not come.

This was peace and tranquility on the surface. Him on this beach with the palms and fleecy clouds, the surf rolling in.

Underneath, it wasn't close to that.

**

Clint got off the chopper in Buabidi and went to the council building. Naldo and Elena greeted him. He said he was there on a serious matter. A breach of faith by one or both of two people.

"Who has charge of the records of the time when the company was trying to make an open-pit phosphate mine in the comarca? The time when the weapon was used?"

Elena looked thoughtful, then went to the files to check.

"Wilam Flores ... no, he died three months ago. Gloria Comacho."

"I have some serious ... died? How?"

She got another file from another cabinet. "He died from a drug overdose."

"He what?!"

"Dios mio!" Naldo cried. "He did not use drugs! He would not be permitted to have access to any of this if he did!"

Clint stared at the wall for a few seconds. "Do you have records of the people here for the museum at that times? Will there be records of anyone who came to speak with him?"

"Of course," Elena answered. "We use the system in the offices you had installed. Everything is on memory sticks. Even videos."

"I'll need for three days before he died. Maybe longer, but that should have it."

She went to a rack with thousands of small cubbies to look at the dates noted on each in a section marked "Consultants – Wilam Flores" to hand Clint three memory sticks. She pointed to a computer in a small cubicle. He went to boot up and insert the first.

There was a list of names and times. None seemed to be in any way familiar.

The second had Dr. Karl Franken, Elsa Jones and Daniel Helper - 3:30PM.

He brought up the time on the memory stick. Peabody, Holden and the Dr. Franken on the other video.

They discussed the museum a moment, then Franken produced a paper to hand to Wilam, who looked at it and inserted it into a reader, which showed. It was a request to be allowed to inspect the artifacts from the time for a scientific analysis. Flores said he must meet with the council. He felt there would be no problem, so long as the weapon itself was not discussed in any way.

They were to return tomorrow at nine for the answer.

Clint sat back. So the analysis was legitimate. What Peabody and company probably didn't know was that Wilam didn't know anything at all about the weapon.

He put in the next memory strip. 9:00. They were waiting in the office. Wilam came in and said Dr. Franken was granted one half hour to study the materials. He gave them the copy of the comarca video. Peabody and Holden could not attend.

The next morning Wilam was found in his house, dead of an overdose of drugs. Several. Scopolamine was one of them.

So. They followed him home and drugged him, but he didn't know diddly-shit about the weapon. Clint thought. *They were now murderers. I have to find Franken to know if he was part of that.*

He went back to the second stick and brought up the request, It was from a scientific committee in Panamá City. It was signed by Emilio Bouher, recording secretary. Physical Science Advisory Committee International.

They were safe to that point. No one had the weapon now except JK.

He called JK and told him what had happened and what he now expected.

Then he headed for Panamá City.

***

JK called CD and told him what Clint reported. He had suggested that CD and Nick find where Franken was while Clint investigated that committee. There were records of such a committee, but it was a little nothing thing, so far as he could find. It was all too possible it was something set up for future use, when and if needed.

CD agreed. He could get cooperation from immigration because Clint had vouched for him. Clint had enough to do to try to find what was behind the whole thing. He suspected he knew.

"Uh-huh," JK replied. "It's exactly what I suspected from the first. Peabody was a total fool to try to pull that bluff. I can't understand why she would do anything that stupid."

"You know something? Franken was sent by that committee."

There was a short silence. "So Franken was sent to learn if there was an authentic danger. He determined there was. He didn't know they didn't get any information about the weapon. Peabody's major mistake was in letting her ego make her think she was in control. She didn't have any insurance. Exit the lovely lady."

"She thought Holden was her insurance. That would have worked ten percent of the time if they weren't together. They were able to take her out and cancel the policy at the same time."

"And it would have worked if Holden were somewhere he couldn't be found – until he was found."

"But you *do* have the weapon. We'll have to use that."

Nick considered something. He wondered if Clint and CD had come to the same conclusions. The bluff was exactly that. That she didn't have the weapon was shown when that video was taken with her holding a silly movie prop. If seeing the weapon would show people what it was, no such video would exist. There would have been a video of her using the weapon, but the weapon wouldn't be shown. This was, as in one of Dave's books, an ocean liner in a puddle.

He considered things. It still left a huge problem for the world. That same bunch of throwbacks was in charge. Maybe a way to pry a little of their control from them could come from it.

That would occur to CD and Clint.

And to JK.

He turned back. He would go out to the island and help with the house and gardens. He liked working with these people. They were real and basic.

He was going to find contentment here – and more.
**

Clint got off the chopper and headed for the address the police had given him for the home of Emilio Bouher. It was in a semi-upper class section. There was a four year old Honda in the drive.

He went to the door to call, "Buenos!" That was the same as knocking in the USA.

A rather pretty girl answered. He said he was Clint Faraday and asked to speak with Sr. Bouher. She opened the door and invited him in.

Inside, the house was luxurious. There were antiques and paintings and statuary. He was led to a den with more of the same. It had a big mahogany desk and a lot of modern computer equipment.

A thin dark man with flecks of grey in his black hair seated behind the desk waved to a seat.

Clint raised an eyebrow.

"I expected you. You are known as tenacious."

"You couldn't figure it was a bluff when that silly video showed her with that super ray gun from a Will Smith movie?"

"I was stupid not to see that. It is a good thing to know that no one has the weapon. That was a matter of the deepest concern to a great number of people."

"Someone does have the weapon. The Indios can have it at anytime they feel it to be necessary. There's one person who has several made because of this shit."

"Shit is what it is. Dr. Franken says it could be that or a highly directed laser, which can be reflected. I choose that explanation."

"I see. Perhaps I can arrange a demonstration that will prove it's no laser. We don't have nearly the capacity to make that small a hole at three miles. It would absorb tremendous power, which the Indios don't have. No one could make a directed laser at home."

"We have only the one person who claimed that, and he's conveniently dead."

"You're rather stupid, aren't you? You didn't check with the police lab about their inspection of those holes in planes? From the middle of the comarca, where there isn't any major power generator? You think a few solar cells could power a laser that would do that at three miles?"

Bouher stared at the desk for a few seconds. "I'm no scientist."

"Neither is Franken if he says that could have been done with a laser."

"Dr. Franken says the crap about time distortion and gyroscopic effects and some kind of logarhythms is just that. Crap." He looked a little shocked.

"We knew about the bugs. We used them. *Part* of it *is* crap."

"Part of it?"

"Uh-huh."

"You know what the weapon is?"

"Me? No. JK does. He made a couple to test. He says the best way to throw what pass as scientists today off is to make ridiculous statements, along with a few facts. Determinant logarhythms? Bullshit! Reject the whole thing!"

Bouher stared at the desk again. "We have to stop this!" he whispered.

"You almost brought it," Clint pointed out. "Your type of people who run the world through a lot of greedy schemes can't see that having more than a certain amount is always negative? What's the point? It's totally empty. You *know* that, but you keep on."

"You give away millions. You don't want something for yourself? For your children?"

"But we *have* it all! Can't you see that? We don't hide from anyone. We have friends. Actual, real friends. We hug when we meet. I care about them, they care about me. No one gives a shit about you, you don't give a shit about anyone."

"You don't make sense. Everyone wants more, wants control, wants power!"

"You're a dinosaur. You're about to bring about your own extinction if you can't see what you are. I'm like the Indios. I pity you. It's all right here, but you can't see that.

"Are the idiot four part of you or just puppets you use?"

"I can buy as many thousand like them as I choose."

"Okay. That's all I wanted to know. Sit here and rot away among all this fabulous art and money. It's for nothing. Those things have to be shared to have any meaning. Your life is a huge shitpile of things that amount to nothing and you're not capable of seeing that.

"One warning. A way to bring the weapon out, fast, is to interfere with my people in any way. Wilam is dead because of your interference, if indirectly. If it was directly, you'd be dead now.

"I want to get back to my friends. I have them, you see. You can get back to sitting behind that desk trying to figure how to get more empty, meaningless things. I like to feel my life has some meaning. You don't have that. That's where it is. Goodbye."

He stood up and walked out. Bouher was staring at the desktop.

Back home. No more of this bullshit.

***

CD considered. Clint called and explained what had happened. The kids could all go back home. It was somewhen in the future, not now.

He called JK as soon as Clint said he was on the chopper, heading home. He explained what Clint had done. JK said he had done one thing that he would use. The weapon was things that were found around the house or garage. You could go to a garbage dump and

Page 125

get enough of most of it to build fifty of the things. All you needed past that was some copper wire and a battery of some sort.

They chatted. The families were having a lot of fun on the islands. He would tell them they could go back home, but were welcome to stay for as long as they liked. Things in the world were on the brink of crisis, but that's what those people manipulated the situation to be. They made so much *money* from it!

CD rang off, sealed the jet, and headed for the island. It would be good to be there. He would leave the rest of the world to its own fate and problems.

JK

JK put a thing together from PVC pipe, some aluminum pie plates, a circular TV antenna, some capacitors and resistors he took from an old computer, and a neon light starter coil. It looked like a Rube Goldberg thing.

Psychology: Rube Goldberg's things always worked, if for silly reasons.

He took it out to a terrace and put the weapon behind it, extending through the center. He took a one inch thick piece of iron plating and put it against the wall, then went to the contraption to hook up a motorcycle battery to two copper wires that went to the device in the rear. The process from when he took the plate to lean against the wall was on unbroken video that followed him everywhere through a director on his belt.

He went to check the wiring, showing a tantalising piece of the device, but not enough to actually show anything. He picked up a small round rock from a flower bed and dropped it into a piece of ½" PVC that extended above the back of the device.

He went back to stand in front of the device to the side where both the device and the plate were in the picture. He punched a button on a switch he had in his hand.

He went to the plate and showed the hole through it, holding it up so the sunlight showed it was all the way through, then went to the wall. It was constructed of rocks that were about two feet thick. He ran a piece of wire through the hole in the rock. It went all the way through.

He went back to turn the device off, then went inside to take the video recorder, recording the whole thing, to his computer room.

He had an unbroken cycle recorder on the video. There was no way it could have been faked.

He sat to make a voice recording that would explain everything except what the weapon was.

He added a warning at the end of it.

The house was done. It fit the place perfectly. It was simple, but complete.

Alma came from the orchid garden with Tyna. Nick and Janet came from the dock to stand with Clint and the others to look out over the water toward the comarca on the shore.

"We're here. Paradise," Janet said. They all agreed..

Nick's cellular rang. He answered, after saying he meant to get rid of that damned thing.

It was Pancho. He was back in Florida. Things were, if not great, a lot better than recently. The world situation had relaxed a bit. He thought it was because of something JK did. Everybody had gone back to wherever their home was except Tony and Shirley Jacobi, who decided they would spend half their time on JK's island and half elsewhere.

They all chatted with Pancho, then went inside where Natalia and Yveth surprised them with a feast that would have cost five hundred dollars a plate anywhere else if the ingredients were even available.

They lazed around for an hour, then went for a swim in the Caribbean, then rinsed in the river to return to the house. Clint's phone rang, this time. He noted there were six missed calls. From Rojelio.

"Yo, Ro! Wa-apping?"

"Greetings, Clint. I have a small mystery here. A tourist who died when she fell off a small cliff. The problem is that there was no reason for her to be there."

"Would you care to investigate a bit?"

Clint didn't hesitate. "No."

Clint Faraday Mysteries
Book final
Death Closes the Case
© 2015 by C. D. Moulton

Clint is old and can't move around like he used to. He feels useless because he can't work with his people much.

He still can solve mysteries!

This one involves a lot of people. Innocent bystanders. It is a scheme being run by very powerful people.

Can the famous Clint Faraday find a way to end this threat to his people?

Contents

Clint Faraday, retired PI from Florida, USA, now living on the comarca Ngobe Bugle in Panamá, rubbed his swollen knee and grunted. It was getting to the point where he couldn't function well when any physical action was required.

He had been exceptionally lucky for most of his life. He was always healthy and able. Now, at 89 years, it was catching up with him. He had to accept the simple fact that he couldn't run around like a twenty year old anymore. When he hurt himself, he stayed hurt. He didn't heal at a tenth the rate he used to.

He was fortunate that he still had his mental facilities. He could still solve a puzzle.

He had become expert on finding information on the internet. He just recently had run down a scheme by a bunch of sleazy politicians to take some of the comarca land where they would build casinos and hotels on the pristine beaches on the Caribbean. They had bribed some top people in the government to declare the land was national land that was open for ROP settlement that could be filed upon and title purchased after two years. The files were backdated to allow the scum to start building as soon as the title was cleared, which would have taken 45 days.

It was comarca land. The whole thing was a scam to steal the land. An old story. Clint knew how that one worked and was able to have three big names jailed for two years on corruption charges and have two big mobsters deported. The comarca land was re-certified.

It was hushed up to a great extent by the corruption in the courts and police. That was part of the scheme.

He didn't have to leave his house on the island just out from Cusapín for that. The reason he was still alive was because he was living on the comarca, was declared Ngobe, the second person to ever be accorded that honor, and the comarca wouldn't allow anyone to go to where he was. The Indigenos take care of their own.

Tyna, his younger wife, still a beautiful woman at 67 years of age, came with a glass of guanabana chicha.

"Nito (their son, now head of police on the comarca) called and said to tell you to stop acting like a teenager," she said. "I told him I've tried to get that through to you for thirty or forty years."

She laughed, along with him.

He sighed and asked if Nicole had called yet. She was heading the hospital on this end of the comarca.

"She said she has you scheduled to meet with Dr. Schrader in Bocas day after tomorrow. Dr. Salardes studied under him. He's a specialist about aging."

"Huh! I age. I'm almost ninety, so I have to slow down. I've been slowing down 'til I'm sick of it! I can't even go to the garden to dig yuca anymore! I'm becoming a useless drag on you and the people!"

"Don't be ridiculous! You just saved more than five hundred hectares of comarca land from being stolen! That's hardly a drag on the people! It's as far from useless as you can get!

"As for me, I can't picture life without you. You're my happiness and my reason for going on. You and the kids.

"Nicole is pregnant. Mathilde says it will be a healthy boy she will name Carlos Faraday Jimenez."

"And Nito named his kids Tyna and Guillermo Faraday Vega. The Faradays are going to be like Smith in a few generations, I think.

"Why Guillermo?"

"Because Guillermo is still a prize gigolo stud at fifty eight years of age. You know how Nito is about sex."

"Yeah. Do I have to go to Bocas?"

"You promised."

"Shit!"

It was known far and wide that any promise made by Clint Faraday would be kept. Period. Pass me a beer.

"When do I have to be there?"

"Day after tomorrow at ten o'clock. We can go to Bocas tomorrow afternoon. Judi says our house there is vacant right now, so we can go directly there."

"If I have to, I have to. Shit!"

Clint tied to his dock at Bocas Town on Isla Colón and waved to Judi Lum, the attractive Oriental woman who had helped him with his cases when he first came to Panamá. She was in her early seventies and was still a striking woman. She still ran the hospital and clinic construction on the comarcas. Clint had made millions of dollars as a detective, mostly by accident. She came over as Tyna was unpacking their clothes for the next few days.

"Hi, Jude! Anything new and different here?" Clint greeted.

"Same old same old. Same old crooks with new faces – along with most of the old faces. The sixth street crowd has moved over past the airport, which is good. The police can watch them a lot easier. You know that Jim died last year. Tom came whining back from Ecuador and proceeded to get his ass kicked twice in

one week. He decided to go back to Vermont or wherever."

Tom was a pain in the ass type who knew everything
there was to know about anything. His only trouble was
the parts he got wrong, such as the facts. He gossiped
about people and got into trouble with it. He refused to
learn.

"Couldn't happen to a more deserving person," Clint
replied. "What happened with Manny?"

"Manny Matthews" was actually Marko Bocinni, a
major crime syndicate head from California who Clint
had established on Isla San Cristóbal. He had been a lot
of help in Clint's cases because of his power and
connections in the underworld. He had worked with
Clint and Judi with the hospitals and clinics and was a
respected pillar of the community. He had made the
mob go legitimate. It was his father who has been the
big mafia don.

"He developed a serious lung problem and moved to
somewhere in the Mediterranean – like we told people
he did thirty five years ago. He can't take the humidity
here in a rain forest. His kids are taking over the stuff
here. They're a lot like he is. It's good to know things
will stay the same with our projects.

"There is one problem that nobody knows about,
though. I heard some things and had Tony check them
out through his dad. Something's afoot here that could
be bad news for everyone."

Judi was the best information gatherer Clint ever
knew. She could drop a word or phrase into a conversation, get an answer, act like she didn't hear it and
was talking about something else anyway, and find

things in an hour it would take Clint and detective methods a month to find.

"What sort of thing? I'm not doing the detective bit anymore. I can't get around well enough to be playing that part."

"It affects the comarca in some way I haven't learned yet. Politics."

"We just solved that one. They're gone!"

"No. Maybe some of the same people, but something different, something the CIA might be behind. I think it has to do with that big copper lode and some other minerals they found with the satellites."

"Well, I'll try to stay out of it. I might do some tracing with the comps and such. Maybe I'll find something."

"Yeah. CD and Alma and Nick and Janet take lessons from Clint in that part of it," Tyna said. "Clint has to be careful. There are some scary people around lately."

"These are mostly Panamanian. You know how the CIA works," Judi warned.

"Brother! Do I!"

They chatted for awhile. Judi and Tyna went to town to get a few groceries. Clint turned on his computer and checked out what he could find, then went into town to see who was still around. He didn't know many of the present bunch.

He was going past The Reef as two men were going in. One was a man Clint caused to be thrown out of Panamá ten years ago as an undesirable. He was involved with a plot to steal an Indio's land out past Puerto Armuelles. The other was a judge from Chiriqui. A judge who was under suspicion of corruption a few years ago.

Suddenly Judi's hints looked like they could stand a wee bit better investigation.

Milton Forbes turned just then and spotted Clint. He said something to Judge Raul Rancheros, who turned to stare.

Clint had exceptional peripheral vision. He didn't appear to look at them. Rancheros shook his head, then looked confused, then shrugged.

So. They weren't certain it was him. That could be a plus.

Clint kept walking. They went on inside the restaurant.

This was getting interesting. Clint wasn't in a position where he could learn anything at the moment, but he was damned well going to learn some things.

He went on back to his house. Tyna and Judi were cooking up one of the recipes they learned about years ago. He said Forbes and Rancheros were in town. He wanted to know what they were up to. No matter what, it was to no good. Not those two! The women agreed.

He fired up the computer and sat back to think. He had to have a reference point to start an investigation.

Okay. Judi said copper and such. That had been going on for about fifty years. The government kept trying to take the Indigeno land. They would open-pit mine and leave a huge scar on the Earth that would last centuries. The Indios wouldn't permit it.

Milton Forbes was into that uranium scam, where they were trying to smuggle out enough to build a dirty nuclear bomb.

There was no uranium in the area where they were trying to get in. Forbes probably had the connections to handle other vital metals.

Rancheros was just a corrupt judge. He would have the setup that would allow stealing land, but the comarca wasn't exactly a smart place to try it. He would try to nationalize the land – which wouldn't have much chance, either.

But Judi said the CIA was involved. That could mean a very big problem for everyone. Their record for doing anything positive was non-existent, almost.

Find out who else is involved. All he could do now was hypothesize. That was a fast track to nowhere.

How corny!

He called Tony, Marko's oldest son. Tony said he would get the organization to check things out.

Clint sat back to think. It was a matter of waiting until he had more information. If there was a company or engineer involved it would give him a place to start.

Forbes and Rancheros had seen him. They would check to find he was there.

Clint went to a box of computer parts and accessories to take out several spycams and audio pickups. He had places to put them where not an inch of the inside of the house would be missed. He took out a backup computer and put it into the little space he designed to hide it. He hooked up everything and tested it.

He was called to dinner. It was delicious.

Judi and Tyna would go into town to visit friends. Clint said he didn't feel like walking that much, so he'd stay around there and work with the computer.

He didn't want to scare them, so didn't tell them about the basic precautions he was taking. He did make a note about the system and where the comp was that ran the surveillance and so forth. He put it in the files under household expenses in the folder for gas and electric. Judi knew about that because they'd used the method to trade information when they felt the house was bugged or worse. Even when he went back to Cusapín he could let her know to check it regularly. The system worked on sound and motion activation as well as breaker beams and such.

He then took a cold Balboa Ice out to the deck to sit watching the bay at sunset.

This was a peaceful place. The town, two minutes walk away, was a typical Caribbean tourist trap, but here, this close, it was quiet and tranquil.

He wanted it to stay that way.

The phone rang, so he groaned out of the chair and answered it.

"Mr. Faraday? I wish to know what you are doing here. You will tell me, because I am sitting in the park not fifty feet from your wife and neighbor."

Clint had to bite his tongue to stop himself from saying what he thought at that moment.

"I have a doctor's appointment in the morning. It isn't any of your business. If you threaten me or my wife or my friends or my people in any way you have gone too far. There's no going back.

"Who are you and what do you care where I am or what I'm doing?"

The caller hung up. Clint had to control his temper. He was sure that was Forbes. The gringo accent and phraseology told him that.

Wasn't it?

It was a gringo with an education. If it wasn't Forbes it was someone in his group.

Why didn't he speak in English? Rancheros and Forbes certainly knew it was his native language. Both spoke English.

It wasn't Forbes. Forbes' Spanish wasn't quite that good. It wasn't Rancheros. Rancheros' was a lot better.

Whatever and whoever, they had threatened Clinton Faraday's wife and a friend. They started out by going too far.

They were going regret doing that. Bitterly!

The doctors probed and twisted and yanked at him, then came to the decision that he was getting older and had to adjust his life to that fact. He was in better shape than most people who were in their sixties and had taken care of themselves.

He wouldn't heal as fast. He was lucky in that he always ate natural foods, so calcium wasn't taken out of his system. His skeletal structure was exceptionally good. His eyes and ears were very good, far better than most in their sixties. He was still able in the sexual parts, though his prostate was slightly enlarged. No hint of cancer there. No signs of Alzheimers. No liver deterioration. Unclogged arteries. A small shadow on the MRI, but it probably wasn't too serious, though it was in an inoperable spot in his brain. They would have to watch it. He would come back in one week for a follow-up.

So he would owe them a couple of hundred bucks to tell him what he already knew. It would make Tyna feel better, so it was worth it for that. She was his most basic care nowadays. If there was one worry he didn't have, it was money. He still had over eight million dollars in the bank, though he had given the comarca and friends a lot of millions, particularly in building schools and hospitals and such.

He got back to the house at ten to six. Tyna left a note to go to Ben's place for dinner, so he checked the comp surveillance. Nothing.

He walked to Ben's for the gourmet meal.

Ben Longstreet was a gay man who had been a friend since Clint moved to Panamá. Earl, his lover, came a bit later. They had been a couple since.

Dinner was large shrimp stuffed with a crabmeat and vegetable filling, breaded, and deep fried in olive oil with a bit of garlic, a salad made of lettuce, pineapple, maraschino cherries, and white grapes with a light dressing Earl whipped up. Steamed broccoli and cauliflower in a cheese sauce and good old French fried potatoes. Dessert was guanabana ice cream, homemade.

They discussed only pleasant things during the meal. After, Clint managed to bring up the fact Forbes and Rancheros were in town. Ben had seen them, but just walking on the street. They were with some lawyer from David or somewhere.

Clint and Tyna went back to the house for the night. Judi and Ben and Earl went into town.

Tyna and Clint puttered around, fixing things that needed fixing. They went to bed a little after midnight and were up with the dawn, as usual. Tyna said she was anxious to get back to the island. A day was plenty of Bocas Town for her! It wasn't so bad, now that so much had moved to Boca del Drago, but she liked home. BT would never be home.

"Judi will go with us. She likes the island and wants to see Alma and Janet," Tyna said. "She can be ready anytime we say. I told her it would be early."

Clint grunted, then went to the comp. He had a couple of answers from Tony. The lawyer with Rancheros, Forbes, Robinson and Flores was someone named Penceros, from near Frontera.

Penceros? That sounded familiar.

He checked his names list on the comp. Penceros was tied up in that corruption case in Frontera. He was a sleazeball with a lot of excuses for everything he did. It was always somebody else's fault.

They were looking for more financing. What it was wasn't clear, but Tony could get an operative from the old mob to act interested in investing in something that would turn enough profit for a few unreported funds to be added without anyone noticing. They were all crooks, so would respond to another crook.

It had to do with land, but not the land itself. It wasn't stated anywhere in a way that would tell them anything.

"Ty, I'm staying here for a few days. You and Judi can go. I have to check out some things. I think there's going to be a lot of trouble for the comarca if we don't put an end to it. I want to know what those crooks are up to."

Tyna knew it would be pointless to try to change his mind. She warned him that he didn't have the police here on his side nearly so much as in the past.

"I think, with the ones here, the police would be a bad place to depend on. Those are the type who own some higher-ups in the courts and police."

"Well, be careful. You can't go running around like you used to."

"That's what the doctors said. I have to slow down. I think I can find out a few things and have Tony handle anything that needs handling."

She nodded, sighed, and said she'd take the boat over to pick up Judi. Keep in touch. If it gets dangerous, come home. Let Tony handle it.

He nodded. He helped her and Judi pack the boat and kissed her goodbye when they left.

As soon as they were gone he grabbed the phone and made a call to a woman he knew, a woman who was now head of the news department on a very popular TV network.

"Juliene? Clint Faraday here. Care to help light a fire under a few really big slimewad crooks? It could get damned dangerous. Possible CIA involvement."

"Clint? I haven't heard from you in ten years! I'm in!"

"We have to have a way open to be able to get a lot of publicity fast. That means moving before they get a foothold. Here's the basics and what I think might work.

"First, we collect a lot of...."

Clint went to sit in the Golden Grill. He had been going there for more than thirty years. There was a group who were always there for breakfast and coffee and chat. He had stayed around the comarca and went to David a few times the past five years. He had quit the detective bit to a great, extent except when the comarca, his people, needed him.

Penceros was sitting at a table in front and almost fell off the chair when Clint came to say "Buenos dias!" Clint had saved him from a big jail sentence with the promise he would straighten up his act. If he went back to his old ways, he would pay a high price.

"Faraday?! I thought you'd be dead by now! I wouldn't ... I mean, it's good to see you're still active!"

"Not very anymore. It creeps up on you. I stay around the comarca most of the time. It's a lot more tranquil than here or David, and I don't spend so much time in Tula. I can't take a six kilometer hike up the mountains every time I need food or such. Give me the flat ground.

"How are things with you? Keeping busy?"

"Er, um, yes, more or less. I'm checking out investment properties and that kind of thing."

"Too late here. It's done. Maybe around Chiriqui Grande, but that's not the best place anymore. More in Chiriqui. Frontera to Puerto Armuelles is growing fast. There's still some property there that could be a good investment. Most of Tierra Oscura is national land that they can't hope to work around for that kind of development."

"It's beginning to shift away from the coast and deeper into the mountains, but a lot of that is in permanent preserves. They're finding some ... things.

"I have to meet an appointment. Good to see you!"

He got up and left. Clint smirked. He wondered if Penceros knew just how bad a slip he'd made there. They'd found something. The scam artists had something they could turn into a lot of money ... or ... they could make a lot of money by claiming they found something.

He would have to find which. He called Tony to ask him to listen around, then called Juliene to say she should check the files to see what was reported that wasn't reported about a few areas.

"Reported but not reported? Like pressure to bury it or that didn't have enough backup?"

"Yeah."

"Ahh! Both."

"Uh-huh. I'm trying to find a reason."

"Inland and in the higher mountains. Fortuna or the comarca?"

"I think anything in La Fortuna is already found, if it's that big a thing."

They chatted awhile, catching up on things. Clint soon was sitting drinking coffee and thinking. He knew where there were several things they could be interested in, but they were in the center of the comarca, more or less. Amethyst (Book 50: *Where Death Waits*) and gold (Book 33: *Die Trying*) were the most likely that he knew about.

It was going to be a matter of tying one of them – or more – to those things they could use as a basis for a scam. They might also think they could actually mine them.

Not likely. The gold was in a place that was as inaccessible as you could want. The amethyst was, too, when you considered it.

But you could take pictures of it and ... the gold. It had to be that, because no one could hope to live to take pictures of the amethyst.

There could be other things. If the people in the comarca knew about them they wouldn't mention them. They have little or no importance to comarca life.

It wouldn't be the phosphate (Book 19: *A Moving Target*) because that was in relatively flat land near the Caribbean. It wouldn't be uranium (Book 11: *See You in Hell*). That was in Chiriqui Province, near Puerto Armuelles, There was some silver there, too. It was a lot closer to Volcan Barú.

Silver could be in the other mountain areas. There was zinc and lead and some cinnabar. Very secondary considerations. Topaz and jade were tertiary considerations.

Oil was a scam, but everyone knew that.

Clint went over everything in his mind, the locations and conditions in which it was found.

It had to be silver, but what was known wasn't from the comarcas.

But it was known. Not new finds.

Crap! There was a lot of silver that was made into trinkets – a long way from where the known mines were. Not far into the comarca. East of La Fortuna and west of the peninsula where he was staying where Cusapín was the tip. It could be arranged to enter from national land at Fortuna, which was actually comarca land. It was mountainous and several things were there, mostly smaller lodes.

Was the CIA bit a diversion? Was it not involved at all?

Clint remembered several cases where he came across the CIA. That voodoo queen who thought she could take over the economy of Central America or something as nutcase. (book 7 :*Comedy of Terrors*) The latest he remembered was with that derelict ship (Book 48: *Dead in the Water*). There could be a CIA agent who was looking for personal gain.

He didn't have any other ideas. He was just finishing his coffee when Forbes came in and directly to him.

"What are you doing here, Faraday?"

"Minding my own business. I have a house here, as you very well know. I might ask what you're doing here, seeing you were declared persona non grata by Panamá.

"You, Penceros, Rancheros ... maybe I should look into a thing or two. I was out of the business, but you three ... maybe I will look into a thing or two! I wouldn't have considered it until you came on with this bullshit. I would have gone back to the comarca the day after tomorrow and not thought of it until whatever you're up to hits the news."

"You get involved in this, you won't live to watch the news, old man!"

Clint surprised himself with the speed with which he stood and delivered a good solid right to the jaw of Forbes, who went down on the sidewalk and into the gutter.

"You threatened me and have my answer, dickhead! Don't make the mistake of getting in my face again! Your demise will be the thing on the news!"

A local cop ran up with a drawn sidearm he pointed at Clint. Clint said he would show him the papers that would explain some things and took the folder he carried when he might need it from his back pocket. He got out the paper, which was a commendation and authorization for him to act as a ranking police officer anywhere in Panamá.

"He threatened me. I responded. I'll let it be a resolved personal dispute unless he wants to take it further."

"You assaulted me right here in public! I damned well will take it further!" Forbes almost screamed. "It's a lie! I never threatened anyone! He's a liar!"

Clint took the mini-recorder from his shirt pocket. "Care to have a charge of making a false statement to an investigating police officer by a person ejected from this country as undesirable?"

Forbes stared at the recorder.

"In addition; I'm over seventy five. You'd better check the laws here about assaulting anyone my age. You get three years automatically for that – if I make a complaint.

"I don't make one, you don't make one. Ball's in your court."

Forbes turned and stalked off. "He was declared undesirable and ejected?" The officer asked.

"Uh-huh. Don't worry about it unless he pulls another stupid stunt like this."

"You're Clint Faraday? My professor at the academy talks about you all the time. He says you taught him most of what he knows. Sergio Valdez."

"We worked a lot of cases together. I think I broke something in my hand when I smacked that asshole idiot."

They talked a minute, then Clint headed for his house. *Apparently, that bunch thinks I know a lot more than I do. I'll have to remedy that.*

His hand really did hurt like hell. He went into the house and wrapped it with a tight Ace Bandage.

There was no action on the spycams. Clint worked for awhile with the comp, then headed for Refugios for a few beers and some talk with the people there. It wasn't the same without Dave and his friends playing music. They had music, but more Latin flavored. Salsa, which Clint didn't care much for.

He went from there to Toro Loco. It wasn't the same either. The better places were relocating to Drago.

Paulo Robinson and Enrique Flores came in. They avoided Clint, but stared at him a lot. He ignored them, so far as directly looking at them went. He kept them in sight with his peripheral vision.

Penceros and Rancheros soon came in. They talked animatedly with Flores and Robinson a bit, then Penceros came to ask if he could have a word.

"Have several. They're small. Have a seat."

He sat. "Mr. Faraday, you have caused some trouble for myself and some friends. I will admit you also helped me when I most needed it.

"We are trying to start a business project here. We don't wish to have competition move in before we're ready to compete, in a manner of speaking. Is that why you're here? To learn what we plan so someone else can grab the idea from us?

"It's a matter of the financing, basically. If there are problems at this point our financing could fall through.

"I know you don't lie. You will either answer me honestly or will not answer. Is that why you are here?"

"No. I came here to a doctor's appointment. I was called on the phone by Flores – I remember his voice – and threatened. I was then assaulted with threats by Forbes.

"Until that time I didn't much give a damn what you were up to.

"The stupid ass threatened me, for which I don't give a shit. He threatened my wife and my friend. For that, I give a hell of a lot more than a shit. Now I'm going to see what you're up to. If it's all that innocent you wouldn't be pulling this crap."

"Mr. Faraday, Flores called you because of what you caused him in the past, not because of anything the rest of us suggested."

"I didn't cause him anything in the past. He caused it.|"

"We look at it differently."

"Yes. You feel that the person who catches you at some slimy crooked deal causes what happens to you as a result. It never occurs to you that getting into the slime was your doing and what happens as a result is your doing."

Penceros sat there in silence a moment.

Clint shook his head. "If you were legitimate you'd simply tell me what you're doing and I'd either agree that it's legitimate or say that it isn't. You make it look like you're up to something crooked that you don't dare tell me about."

"We want to mine an ore that no one here knows about. We're trying to get permits and such set up that will guarantee we don't lose our asses in it."

Clint decided to take a chance. "You aren't getting any permits to mine silver or anything else on the comarca."

He almost fell out of the chair. "HOW DID..!? I mean, what makes you think we're wanting anything on the comarca. I assure you, what we're after won't be on the comarca. That I can say definitely."

"But it is now. I'm not stupid."

"We'll buy the land! That's no problem!"

"You can't buy anything on the comarca. Land isn't for sale there."

"Enough money, they'll change the law."

"Except you don't have half enough money to bribe anyone on the comarca. The museum (Book 51: *Dead Man Talking*) brings in more than a million dollars every three days. It's down a bit now, but it had more than ten years where it did that. The funds in the bank are drawing eight hundred thirty thousand dollars a day. The mines above Quebrada Tula, that aren't operating, could yield several billion dollars and can be carried out with horses where it won't screw up the Earth for a couple of square kilometers. That means you will bribe government officials and legislators and judges. I think you've overestimated the amount of ore there. You won't get your money back."

"Plus you gave them millions. We won't try to bribe anyone on the comarca. You've proven that won't work."

"No we built several millions dollars on schools and hospitals. That's a much different thing. It's to help my people. That's what being Ngobe's about.

"Now you can stop the bullshit and tell me what you're so worried about if everything's so hunky-dory."

Penceros stared again. "You can have some of the partners expelled from Panamá and we can't finish without them. We can't allow that."

"Interesting to see how you stop me if you give me reason."

"They don't care how they do it. You did me a big favor. I don't want any of this. I didn't think you'd ever know anything about it."

"Get away from them."

"You've said, many times, that there are things you get into and can never get out of. It's happened with me. You can't have a place for me this time. I'm in and am going to get out when I'm dead. There's no other way.

"I've suggested that they simply wait. You have to be nearing eighty years old, though you don't look it."

"I'm eighty nine."

"So. I'm sure they'll wait. It wasn't something that has to be done today. We'll simply refrain from doing anything that will cause notice. You have nothing but to have a couple of us expelled. We can be back in very little time. Judge Rancheros is the only one of the partners who is over forty. He's forty three

"Have a pleasant evening, Mr. Faraday." He got up and went to his partners. Clint sat looking thoughtful.

Could he do something to thwart them? They could do nothing and wait for him to kick off and probably could engineer some crooked way to steal everything from his people. That was *not* going to happen.

He was going to get a lot of stuff together that would stop their little plan. He would leave it with Judi and Ben, who would get a lot of publicity with it at the worst possible time.

They had to be unaware he was doing that. They could counter if they knew what he planned.

Clint looked over the papers he'd put in three stacks. It was, first, a record of the times he'd come across those people, the results, and an added form asking why they were there, the ones who were declared persona non grata in Panamá. He scanned the whole package to memory stick and made three copies of it.

The second stack was a record of the times these same schemes were tried and the results. It named the politicians and court officers who had been implicated in corruption cases who were handling the type of transactions.

All of his references were carefully footnoted and sources identified and authenticated. He went to the net to check on the present whereabouts and information on all of them.

Interesting! It seemed there had been three recent deaths among them, including the judge who had declared Forbes persona non grata.

Judge Valdores. He died in a "suspicious" accident. He fell off a third story balcony at his home, landing on the concrete lip of his swimming pool.

Arturo Javeneros M., the person who investigated Penceros and Rancheros originally, was killed in a robbery of a petrol station. He had come into the place when the robbery was in progress and was shot in the head. The robbers escaped without getting the cash that was in a safe the men running the station didn't have a combination for.

Amily Teresa Veras had been electrocuted when the cord on her washer was frayed and grounded to the machine. She was the recording secretary for Valdores.

All within the last two months.

Clint carefully documented the cases and referred directly to the connections. He added the threat Forbes, the one most connected to all three, had made to him and his family, engendering his interest in what the bunch were doing there. He ran the audios from the phone and his recorder into the program. It was a program a man named JK Kiley had made for him. You read until you came to the necessary recording and right clicked on the hyperlink.

He was going to investigate anyone else who died of uncertain circumstances who might have even been peripherally connected to that bunch. Penceros had made a slip when he said there were more than Forbes who had been expelled.

Was Panceros caught in something, as he suggested, and trying to tell Clint a few things?

It was an outside possibility.

The third stack was about the silver and other things in the comarca and the fact that Penceros had stated they were trying to get an illegal permit and to have the land declared national property. He noted that the process wasn't completed and that they had backdated papers to indicate they were users of the property and that they filed for ROP that was to be purchased from the government to be titled.

He carried one memory stick to Ben and Earl, one would go to his Cusapín house to be held by Nick Storie, and one to CD Grimes to be held in case of his own unavailability to finalize the case for any reason.

He was well aware that he couldn't bring any of this forward for more than a request to investigate at this point, and that he would have to admit that it was mostly speculation on his part about what they were doing. All he could hope to do at this point was to get Forbes thrown out of the country. That would leave the others to complete the scheme as soon as Clint Faraday died of old age or whatever.

He laid it out to show it was a criminal conspiracy among a small group, and that they made threats and otherwise acted as a unit.

Now to get something that would tie them up in a way the courts would be forced to act. That would be a matter of getting witnesses to any major part of it. It would have to be solidly tied into the criminal conspiracy or they would produce a goat who would get three or four years and they would be able to complete the plan.

Clint wondered how much Forbes was going to get for sitting in a cell for four years. He would then be expelled ... so. He would be expelled instead of prosecuted. That was why he was here. It was why he had gone to the extremes to get attention while Penceros et al were being reasonable businessmen. While Clint and the police and news media concentrated on him, the others would appear to be embarrassed by him and would be glad that he was expelled because he was making their entirely aboveboard, except for keeping competition unaware that they were working to get a reasonable blah, blah, bullshit, deal done.

They hadn't counted on Clint Faraday getting invol- ved. He had been very quiet for several years, except for the internal affairs of the comarca ... but this was an affair that involved the comarca.

It involved the comarca in the northern part, where Clint hadn't been active in even more years. That's why Penceros was shocked to learn Clint knew about the silver. That was one shot in the dark that hit the target dead center!

The one thing they could not survive was publicity. They didn't think Clint could work that if he didn't have proof of much more than he had. They could still work it with a few corrupt slimeballs that were in the court system. Penceros and, very definitely, Rancheros, would have those contacts set up and ready to go.

He called Juliene. He would be sending the whole thing as it was set up to her personal computer at her home. He didn't want a chance that anyone else would see it. It would tell them he was going after them. It was too soon for that.

"Juli, I'm going to have to solidify the conspiracy part. I want it tied so tight they can't get past that one point. It's the only weak link in that chain! Conspiracy will tie them all to the same anchor chain.

"Do I sound obsequious or what?

"Forbes has to be connected through conspiracy or their scheme might work – except I guaran-damned-tee you they will have every Ngobe in Panamá gunning for them. That will mean bringing in the police, which would bring international publicity that would force Panamá to act against them.

"I don't want it to come to that.

"Damn it! I'm getting too old for this shit!"

"Clint, we have a lot of information in the files about them. I'll dig as deep as I can. Maybe we can come up with more than the unlikelihood they are up to something that's not crooked. If we can tie them together from the time they were in that corruption mess we can add a lot to your case. We have to be able to show a very strong probability. If we can add our own probability to what you're sending we can get it to the point of the fact they're guilty until proven innocent here will act. They can claim one or two, even five things are coincidental. They can't claim ten are!

"If I remember ... Clint! Penceros got a scare because of the terms of him not going to jail if he stayed clean. He almost got caught at that, but it was *Rancheros* who alibied him off the hook! We have a Hell of a connection for the past six years!"

"I love you, Juli! Find anything else and we can tie them all into it! A conspiracy, all are equally guilty!"

"I might have another thing ... Flores. I'm pretty sure there's some connection about a corrupt judge and him. I think just maybe ... Rancheros was in on that. Some character named ... Dunstan? Dunworthy?

"Something like that. Another crumby cheap crook you had expelled so Panamá wouldn't have to pay his room and board in the pen for twenty years.

"I'll research it as close as anything I ever did, Clint. Promise! Those crooks are all tied in one way or another. There aren't really that many, so they're forced to form their own clique. We watch that clique and gather a lot of information that we usually can't ever use.

"Sometimes a piece will fit in one area or another."

They chatted for awhile. Clint was frustrated by what he couldn't do anymore. They agreed to keep in touch. Juli suggested they use a code like they did in that case where Clint disguised himself as his "cousin," Jim Hanrady with any direct contact.

Well, things were going to start moving. Clint just hoped it would be in time to keep it from getting any bigger. He didn't have Marko to gather information the way he used to. Nick and CD were there, but they didn't know enough about Panamanian crooks to do much, plus he wasn't going to involve them in this.

He was going to investigate who else he had expelled from Panamá as undesirable.

Neil Duncaster? A mobster connection who had helped the world out by hitting four other mob thugs? It seemed likely.

He went into Bocas Town for a good meal, then to some of the places he used to frequent. Only a few of the people he knew well were still around. It had been a few years since he spent any time in Bocas. He much preferred the comarca.

Obilio and Silvestre Smith, a couple of very close Ngobe friends (yes, quite a few of the local Indigenos are named Smith, Taylor, Robinson, Bosman, Trotman and such) he had helped at various times, and who were running a very successful food supply business that Clint, Judi and Manny had set up, took him to a new Indigeno bar. He had a pleasant night and went back to his house at about one thirty AM.

He was a little drunk. He didn't drink the beers on the comarca except when he was with special friends.

In the morning he was going to have to start an intense search for information. These four were certainly not the whole bunch in on the scheme. He wanted to tie everyone concerned on that end together. Miss one and it would just be delayed, not stopped.

He intended to see it stopped. He just hoped he would be able to do that. He didn't delude himself about his loss of abilities, at least on the physical end. His mind was still good. He would put it to use.

He was just sitting at the comp when it dinged. E mail from Juliene:

Clint - Pablo Aristes, Mexico, Mob. Connected to Flores. Rancheros dismissed a case against him four years ago when he was caught in a land scam in Veraguas.

So. The thot plickens.

Clint went through the old files on the comp to bring up Aristes. It seemed he was tied up with a Colombian and a Venezuelan in some kind of deal with that Costa Rican (Book 31: *Rest in Pieces*) woman. Laundering, mostly. He didn't know (or care) what the involvement was – until now.

He went on the police net to look up the case. Aristes was into various scams and laundering. He had connections to a Colombian named Quiroz, who died in a vendetta in Medellin. They were into smuggling emeralds out of the country and were caught by Interpol. Quiroz died before he could be called to testify. Typical.

Clint sat back. He was getting a headache, and he never did. He found some aspirin in the medicine cabinet and took a couple. It was probably the different food and stress.

Someone called, "Buenos!" at the front door. He glanced at the spy cam picture on the top of the screen, thought a second, turned on the surveillance system and called, "Pase! Está en la cocina!" (Come in! I'm in the kitchen!)

Penceros and Flores came in a moment later. Clint had put Spider Solitaire on the screen and moved a couple of cards before he looked up.

"Oh! I was expecting someone. What's up?"

"We were passing and wanted to speak with you about a few things," Penceros answered. "I don't know if you know Enrique Flores?"

"We've met. What kind of things?"

"Mr. Faraday," Flores replied, "We are caught in a trap of our own making. Had we known you might become involved we would not have built the trap, but it is done and can't be undone.

"We are planning to mine some ores that are on the comarca, if only a very short distance from national land. We planned to have the area declared national land that was open for ROP possession. We have already made most arrangements and are in possession on the records, if not in actuality.

"Mr. Faraday, it is in a part of the comarca that no one is using, and that no one would be using for many years, if ever. It harms no one, and we would compensate the people there.

"Enrique suggested that we come here to explain. He says you are concerned for the damage to the comarca and the Ngobe. This does no harm. We will restore the land when we have mined the ores. That will be on the contract.

"Other partners, the ones with the power, do not see it that way. They have always taken what they want. This would be no different. They will try to take the land through the planned method. They would agree to only a small compensation to the people of the comarca.

"We are in the trap because of our involvement with those people in the past. We can't escape and live. It is that simple.

"Mr. Faraday, this would not harm the people of the comarca."

"You're both lawyers. You both know perfectly damned well what a precedent is. It would establish a precedent in law that would become a major taking of comarca land. Don't try to hand me a line of BS that a ten year old could see through."

"Mr. Faraday ... I know that would seem to be so, but we will make it a special case exception that could not be used in such a manner," Penceros insisted.

So! That's what they want! A precedent that would destroy the comarca over the years!

"A precedent would be the foot in the door," Clint argued. "Once there, it would always be there.

"Ain't gonna happen while I'm alive to stop it!"

"Then maybe there's another solution to our problem? Hmmm?" Flores hissed.

Clint pulled his Glock from under the computer slide. "Works from either direction, would you say?

"I was planning to go back to Cusapín tomorrow, after the doctors' report. I think maybe I won't!"

Penceros was aghast. "Dios mio! What is the matter with you, Juan Luis!? Dios mio! Mr. Faraday! I swear I'm no part of any such thing! Dios mio!"

"Penceros, I tend to believe you – to an extent. The extent that you never dreamed I would get involved.

"I am, as of this moment, involved. All the way.

"You can't get out, but your value is not here anymore. If anything ... untoward happens to you, it will involve the policia. It will also involve a lot of publicity, which is the one thing your little scheme can't stand up to. It will bring the Ngobe into it to the point none of your partners had ever be anywhere without a dozen or so bodyguards.

"Penceros, get out of Bocas. I would suggest Panamá City is as close as you should ever come until this is resolved."

"I guess that's our only real choice, now," Flores said dejectedly.

"I said Penceros. You threatened me. That makes it personal. I give no corner to the rest of you."

"You don't know who you're dealing with!" Flores cried.

"If Aristes and Duncaster are as good as you can do, you're a thousand kilometers out of your league."

Both Penceros and Flores looked like they'd been kicked in the crotch.

"I suppose you have better ... helpers," Flores said with a sick attempt at a sneer.

"Bocinni? Armakov? You would ask?"

"Dios mio! I warned them! Dios mio!" Penceros cried.

"You're out of it for now. Keep it that way," Clint said to him, then turned to Flores. "You were leaving."

Flores and Penceros left. Clint was damned glad he had that system on! Here was a video of Flores making a threat on his life!

"That little detail's going to smack you in your obsequious puss!" Clint mumbled.

He ran the video/audio surveillance onto a memory stick and made the three copies. He put the copy for the records into the safe.

"If I have to walk up and blow the brains out of every one of you, so be it!" he said to the wall. "I'm over seventy five. The police can hold me no longer than four hours.

"They can put me under house arrest, but my house is in Cusapín. Even if they can make it here, who cares? If I go to the comarca I'm no longer under Panamanian law.

"I have options you never considered!

"I'm hungry and talking to myself. Shit!"

He went into the kitchen to warm up some lobster chowder from the freezer.

Things were going to get interesting now. They would figure he wouldn't go after Forbes, so their distraction wouldn't work. That didn't leave a lot of options open for them.

He had to keep them thinking he knew a lot more than he did. Manny was in the Med and Tony simply didn't have the savvy of the old mob connections. Armakov, he didn't want involved. The Russian mafia were not people you could figure in critical times. They were, to Clint's way of thinking, a long way from sane, though Vasily and Ivan were far more reasonable than many.

If he had to, he had to. Whatever it takes.

He warmed up a double portion of frozen chili and sat on the deck to think and eat. He was tired. Part of getting older. A few years ago he could go at this pace for weeks on end.

Another sign of age. "When I was younger...."

Too bad there wasn't an alternative that appealed to him.

He called Tyna and talked for half an hour or so. Judi heard the name, "Carlos Selasia" mentioned in conjunction to Rancheros. She didn't know if it meant anything.

"It damned well could! He was in some kind of scheme to consolidate crime syndicates in Central and South America," (Book 52: *Killer Deal*) Clint replied. "Shit! There were people from several countries involved in that mess!"

It looked like things would get a lot further than interesting. Try scary as Hell on for size!

Clint was wondering how deep this crap went. He also had to wonder what it was really about. A silver lode worked with some of the people involved, but Selasia brought in a whole new perspective.

He would not be involved in a silver mine, real or scam.

Clint sat at the computer to get in touch with Manny. He no longer had the connection with Interpol.

Armakov did not like Selasia. not even a little bit. Maybe he would have some information. It had been eight years since they had any contact, but they got along well.

He asked if Manny had kept an eye on Selasia. Did he know what he was up to?

Clint: Selasia is in a bad spot with Habenaria (Mex) and Marks (Argentina) at the moment. He wouldn't be involved in anything that might bring his name up. His bout with Rancheros was over a deal where he was caught with forty or so cases of contraband cigarettes brought in through Costa Rica. He bought his way out. Rancheros was the judge who dropped the case for insufficient evidence. That they had forty cases of contraband seized from a truck owned by Selasie, with petrol chits signed by him, being delivered to a warehouse owned by him, with two witnesses who testified he gave them money to be given to Mendez, a tobacco dealer in C.R. wasn't sufficient evidence in a country where you are guilty until proven innocent. I have this lovely swamp in a garbage dump I'll sell cheap!

It was a dead end. A coincidence.

Wasn't it?

Clint looked up Vasily Armakov's number and called. Vasily was in the hospital, critical. Heart. Ivan, his brother answered.

"Clint, Selasia's cut out of anything anymore. He's a mouth-running pain in the ass punk. He gives you any stupid shit, let me know. Tomorrow, no Selasie, so no problem."

"Thanks, Ivan. If he's not involved in whatever the Hell Pencerous and Rancheros are doing, I couldn't care less what else he's into."

"Penceros? That schumpth in Fronterra?"

"Yeah. He's with a group, not by his own choice, if you believe him, that's trying to steal some Ngobe land."

"That silver mine thing? We looked at it. Not likely any deal can be made with the comarca. That museum in Soloy brings in more than anything other than the canal. They can't buy anybody on the comarca, so they won't ... Rancheros.

"They gonna grab the land through the court?"

"They plan to try."

"Then they have backing. If you can find that, you can stop it. Maybe. If you don't, it won't end."

"What I'm afraid of. I want to tie the backing to them and get the whole bunch. I don't have forever anymore."

"Yeah. I'm just celebrating my seventy fourth. You're even more ancient.

"I'll see what I can find. I don't think it's anyone from Panamá, which could mean trouble."

"Thanks, Ivan."

They chatted a minute about things, then Clint rang off.

If Selasia was out of it, it was probably not from Central or South America. Maybe Mexico, maybe the states.

He had to get information, and he had to get it in a way they wouldn't know about it. Only one person he knew could do that.

He called Judi.

They talked about it. Most of the group were in Frontera and David. Chiriqui. He would have to go there to find out where the information might be. He was *not* going to Panamá City!

They made a plan. It would be a lot like old times.

James Arnaz, a man who looked a lot like Clint Faraday – except he was a bit heavier and sported a moustache and walked with a slight hitch, and slowly, gave the butt of the Cuban Cigar a disgusted look and tossed it into the gutter in front of the pawn shop where he had just pawned a stereo system for a tenth of its value. He went to the Ciudad de David Hotel to ask if he had received any mail. They explained (for the fourth time) that he would have to pick it up in General Delivery at the post office.

He sighed and went out to walk the five blocks to the post office. He went to the window where people were mailing things and was told to go to the window by the door. He went there to ask if there was any mail for James Arnaz.

There was a registered letter. He had trouble with Spanish, but was able to show his passport and stamp, so he got it.

It contained a cashier's check for ten thousand dollars.

He went across the street to Banistmo bank. They would cash it, but he had to wait three days for it to clear, seeing it wasn't issued from a Panamanian bank.

"CitiBank is in Panamá!" he complained. The door guard told him where the CiutiBank branch was, so he walked another six blocks to get to the CitiBank. They cashed the check and warned him not to carry that kind of cash around.

He didn't have anywhere else to put it.

"You say you are staying at the Ciudad de David? They have a safe for their clients."

He took a taxi to the hotel, deposited the cash in the safe, went next door to the pawn shop and got his stuff back. It cost him twenty bucks for two hours. Shit!

He put the stereo in his room and went to the restaurant, saw it was too early to eat, so went to his room to watch TV.

His Indio friend, who worked in the restaurant, said the only people who seemed the kind he was looking for ate early, then went out on the town every night. They had been there for more than a month. They ate in other restaurants sometimes, but usually were there on Monday and Tuesday nights. They would be in the restaurant at about 6:00.

Mae Matisu went to the lobby desk to ask if her cousin had left a message. She was handed a note, read it, and rolled her eyes at the ceiling.

"Mal noticias?" the desk girl asked. "Oh! You speak some English and almost no Spanish.

"Bad news?"

"I think not so, but probably maybe yes. She has gone to where she went so not to be here so sorry."

"Well, those things happen."

"Maybe it so for real with life being a crap shoot!"

"I speak Mandarin," the bellboy said, in Mandarin.

"So do I!" she replied. "I am from the islands, but my parents taught me Mandarin and Cantonese.

"My cousin was supposed to meet me here. She has to be in a comarca or whatever they call it. I guess I'll have to try to get by on my own. It will be an adventure!"

"There is a woman staying here who speaks the trade language and Mandarin. She s with some people from the United States, but she is Panamanian. They will be in the dinning room at about six or six thirty. If I see you both I will introduce you."

"Oh! Thank you! It will be good to meet other people with whom I can communicate!"

She chatted a moment, then went up to her room. She got on the elevator with Arnaz and two others. Arnaz said, "Three." She said, "Oh! It is to speak the English I can but not too much sometimes. I am Mae."

"Yeah. Not many speak English here and my Spanish smells. I'm Jim, from Oregon."

"Is in Canada?"

"No. The US."

"I was in the US, but only in New York. It is to not like city so big. No people are real."

"I feel the same about New York!"

"Well and good! Maybe it is to meet two who are people today and can communicate some a little!"

She got off on two. Clint went on up to three.

She said, in their code, that there was someone else who she could communicate with. What did she mean?

Clint sat at a table to the side and sat reading the menu, ordered a red wine and studied the list. He really would like local food, but had to stay in character, so ordered a 16 ounce ribeye.

He looked around the room. There were only four others there. It was early. He had the ability to look at things to the side of where he seemed to be looking. His peripheral vision was far more than most.

Several people came in in the next twenty minutes. He was served, and found the steak to be very good.

The group he was waiting for came in. It was several people he'd met on a case. (book 52: *Killer Deal*) who would be, if connected, bad news. This was the group involved with Selasie.

He had to know if they were connected. He did know they were up to no good if they were involved with anything at all. He was a little worried about Judi. She had met them all in a restaurant in Marioto.

She was in disguise there, too. Not this one.

Judi knew. The comment about two who could communicate was because one of them spoke the trade dialect in Chinese.

Judi carried a broadcasting device. Thankfully, it wasn't the same type as before.

Eight years. Probably safe enough.

The group sat at a table toward the center front. Judi came in and walked by them, not even seeming to glance at them. She took a nearby table not too far from them.

They ordered. The waiter went to Judi, whose mangled Spanish didn't seem good enough to get through to him. She tried English, which she mangled even worse.

Inez Marinera, the woman in the group, called something in Chinese. Judi replied with a slight bit of difficulty. Inez spoke in Mandarin. Judi answered in Mandarin.

Inez invited Judi to join them, explaining to the group that she hadn't had a chance to practice her Chinese in five years. Judi came to the table and was introduced to the group, to which she answered in English. "Mae Matisu. You're welcome and thanks a million times. Very good morning to you all!"

Inez started chatting in Mandarin. Judi did her airhead act. They all ordered beverages and Inez said, in English, that they had ordered the sizzling shrimp dinner.

"Is funny too good! I come to halfway in the ocean and would to eat favorite food from home! Very good wonderful is it!"

"You can tell us if it is really as good and authentic as they claim!" Inez replied. Judi looked lost, so she repeated in Mandarin.

They chatted happily for the truly excellent meal. Clint couldn't very well sit there much longer, so signed the check and went out. Inez looked at him studiously as he passed and said something to Fred Benson. He said he didn't think so. Judi smiled at him as he passed. Inez said something to Judi, who answered.

They ignored him after that. He went to his room to try to listen to what Judi was doing.

Judi went to the restaurant. They were sitting at a table near the center. Clint was to the left a few tables away. She took a fairly close table and acted totally confused with the waiter. Inez Martinera, who she'd met (though

Inez didn't know that) in Mariato, interpreted for her, as she had planned. She was invited to their table.

Inez chatted with her in Mandarin about where she was from and what she came to Panamá for. She said from an island near the China coast, and that she wanted to see the world. She had a cousin who ran a little store in a place called Chiriqui. She was supposed to meet her, but she had been called away for business or something, so here she was, not being able to talk to many.

She was introduced to the other three people, who she knew by sight. They were all involved in the Mariato case.

Clint passed by. She smiled at him.

"Oh? Do you know that man?" Inez asked.

"I spoke to him in the elevator. He seemed nice, but was a little grumpy."

"He looks a lot like a man I knew seven or eight years ago. Clint Faraday."

"His name is Jim Something."

"Hanrady?" Inez seemed very interested, so they knew about one of Clint's disguises.

"Arnite or something. Nitex? Arnaz! He's Jim Arnaz, I think he said. From Canada."

"Oh. Jim Hanrady was from Texas."

They changed the subject. Inez would chat for a few minutes in Mandarin, then would talk to the men in Spanish and English.

The meal was delicious. She said it wasn't like at home. It was better!

Judi took a worked silver and turquoise compact from her purse, then said she didn't know if Panamá was like New York, where she couldn't look at her face at the table, or like back home, where she could.

It contained the sensitive sending microphone, very much miniaturized.

Inez knew about the latest technology. She said it was a beautiful compact and asked to look at it. Judi handed it to her. She opened it and found face powder.

"It was a gift from a man I met. A beautiful man. In a place called La Mina (Very close to the silver lode). I spent a night at his home. He was a very good lover! We communicated, but had no words. It didn't matter," Judi explained. "He made the compact for me. He said there was a lot of silver and turquoise there close."

"He was Latino?" Inez asked.

"No. He was what they call an Indio. An indigenous person."

"La Mina? I hear there is some silver there," Benson said, in English. "It's on the comarca, so only the Indios can get it."

"What?" Judi replied. "It is from there close but not too far. He say it Bugle so he use want whatever but not to other for not Nawbigee or something."

"Then it is on the comarca and can't be mined," Estevez said, in Spanish. "Not enough there to bother with, probably. There are always stories of a find that's got to be the biggest in history or something on the comarca. You can get in on it for ten thousand dollars, but only today because somebody else offered that much. Probably a small lode. Not worth the trouble, but you can make a deal with the man to bring it to you for a price.

"I never did believe any of the stories. They're always a big dream that doesn't happen."

They chatted more, but silver or the comarca or mines didn't come up again. Inez talked about a deal to import liquor at times. Benson always changed the subject.

This bunch wasn't involved. Clint would be happy about that.

Judi finally said she was going to her room. She had to go to Tolé in the morning, then to Bocas, then back home. She asked what her part of the check was. Benson said they invited her, so they would pay the tab. She was good company. It was too bad they couldn't speak with her directly. She was a very interesting and attractive person.

She did the blushing innocent act and left.

"They're out of it," she said to the compact in the elevator.

Clint nodded at the compact, cleaned up, and went to bed. He would still have to find who was financing that bunch and be able to tie it.

"Clint? Tony here.

"You asked to find who was involved with the silver lode. I can't say for sure, but the name John Horvath has come up once too often. He's been in touch with your whole group."

"I never heard of him."

"He's CEO and president of an investment company, on the board of a large drug company, and has a financing project totally in his own name. Out of Houston. Word is that he snacks on sharks for kicks.

"He financed a couple of movies that made a bundle. Those special effects James Bond rip-off things.

"He's a do-it-yourself type who thinks he can do a thing better than you because he's smarter than you."

"In other words, a greedy millionaire with no morals or ethics."

"Sorta. Billionaire. Four, all but five or six million in assets. Five million in cash is enough to squeak by."

"Yeah. I'm down to that, but it will, as you say, get you by.

"Any chance he would come to Panamá?"

"He goes to San Blas at times. He goes to PC at times. He has even gone to David. He's in Seattle at the moment. Has his own private transportation.

"Clint, he might have a tie-in with some people you've come across before. A Faith Somebody who was into a sick hunter game?"

"Faith Richards?" (book 9: *Follow the Blood*)

"Uh-huh."

"Totally emotionless. If he's that sort, this ain't gonna be any fun.

"Thanks, Tony. Horvath may be the only name I need. I have to tie him into it and get him here."

They chatted about the projects, then rang off. Clint sat back, thought, and tried a roaming number in the states that worked ten years ago.

It worked!

"Faith? Clint Faraday here. Remember me?"

"Certainly! How are things, Clint? How are you still alive, as many people as you've had after your ass."

"They can't get to me on the comarca. After awhile, they don't see any reason. I do what I do, they did what they do. There are consequences. That's life."

"Too true! What do you want? Surely you're not calling all the people you know from the past to chat."

"No fooling you! What do you know about a John Horvath?"

"Lousy in bed. Doesn't feel anything and hasn't learned to fake it – like the rest of us. My psycho – logical group.

"I've told him about you. Surely he hasn't gotten in touch with you?

"He wouldn't.

"He might. You'd be a challenge."

"He's into something here that is going to stop. It can hurt a lot of people who *do* feel. Deeply. Me included."

"What can I do – or is this just to confirm what you knew about him?"

"Unless you can tell me how to get him to come to Panamá, it's just for information."

"What'll you do? Blow his brains out? You have to be a hundred by now. Can you handle it?"

"I'm getting awful close to a hundred. If blowing his brains out is the only way, it's the only way."

"I might be able to get him there. I'd like to see you again. Is the promise I would never go to Panamá again still in effect?"

"No. You're an exception. I think you're not a bad person. I didn't always think that way.

"You would get him to come here knowing he might get his brains smeared all over the sidewalk?"

"Sure! Remember how I met you? I might find it amusing. I do feel a minor amusement at times.

"Clint, John likes to think he's smarter than anyone else. He'll go to extremes to prove it. I think I ... how about if I get him, not only to Panamá, but onto the comarca?"

"Could you do that?"

"I think so. I'll offer him a challenge. I'll make him think he's outsmarting the whole damned world! I'll put it to him that there's something that the best criminal minds in the world worked on and failed. He won't be able to resist that!"

They chatted about old times for awhile. She promised she would get Horvath to Panamá – by telling him it might be a one-way trip. He would accept the challenge. He might, as Faith had done, finally find a moment of actual feeling. A thrill.

Clint then sat at the computer and listed everything new they had found. He listed a lot of things that he suspected in a form he could check whether they were true or false conclusions.

He was getting another headache. This crap was getting to him a lot more than he wanted to admit. He was too used to the tranquil life on the comarca. He just wanted this to be over.

"Where are we?" Judi asked. "Any closer to getting it resolved?"

"I think I have a lever. I think I know who's behind it. I might have a way to finish it, but have to depend on a woman whose psychology I simply can't understand."

"Well, Tyna said to make sure you keep the promise to see the doctor today for the follow-up."

"Judi, I want you out of this. It can get a lot more dangerous than you know. There's going to be a person coming after me who I can't figure. He's known to be a totally cold fish. Tony says he snacks on sharks for amusement."

"I've learned to take your advice. I'm out of it. I won't mention it again unless I happen on something I think you should know."

"Fair enough.

"Judi, if ... I want you to explain to Tyna that I'm in something I have no control over. If anything happens to me, I expected it. You don't have to say she was never off my mind from the moment we were married. Never. She and the kids are my first priority, always were, and always will be. She knows that."

"Clint ...?"

"I may not survive this one, Judi. You know I've always loved you as my best friend. If anything happens to ... my family. You're part of my family. We all feel that way."

They were silent for a moment, then Judi nodded her agreement.

"Clint, what's the matter? Really?"

"Judi, I've never had a headache, except when I'd been smacked or something, in my entire life. Now I have a constant one.

"The doctors found a spot in an inoperable part of my brain. They don't think it's serious.

"I think it's serious.

"If I get to where I can't think straight, tell ... no. Call Manny and say to wipe that bunch off the face of the Earth if it's not over by then. All the information and proof is in the memory stick I'll give you. It will be in the recipes, like before."

"Clint...."

"We have to be realistic and we have to be prepared."

She nodded. She reached to touch him. He stood and held her for a long moment. No further words were necessary.

When Judi went back to her house Clint went to the hospital for the doctor to tell him things seemed normal enough. He could tell by the evasions that the doctors had found that things were *not* normal enough.

"Doc, I have an inoperable tumor of the brain. Surely you don't think I can't handle the truth?"

"We don't know enough yet. It my remiss, or it may not. It won't affect you much. You'll get sleepier and sleepier, then one morning you won't wake up. About two months if it's fast, three if not."

"Can you stop the headaches?"

"Yes, to a fairly great extent. I'll give you what we have here and a prescription you can get refilled as much as you feel is necessary. If you overdose it will affect your reaction time and leave you confused. You have to decide on the level that works for you."

He got the rest of the information, thanked the doctors, and went into town to see what was new. It was late enough for dinner, so he went to the Lemon Grass for some Thai food.

The food was very good, but things were just not the same. He remembered when he and Judi and Tyna would come to see their nutty friend, Dave, play with the local talent in the band. All 60's and 70's music, except for the odd request or something one of them wrote.

He went to the golden Grill, but that wasn't the same, either.

Don't get depressed. Not on top of everything else.

He went out a ways to the Indio bar he had come to often in the past. Guilermo was there with Silvio and Obilio. They had a good time.

Then he went home to bed.

The sunrise was beautiful. All golds and pinks. The 1/4 moon was just above the horizon with small fleecy clouds here and there close and a glowing pink band just above. Carenero on the horizon making a dark line between the clouds and water, where the reflections of the colors on the bay were like floating flower petals.

How could such a beautiful serene scene exist in a world with the most disgusting sleaze in control of too many things?

There was nothing to do but wait – but not for long. His time, for the first time in his life, had definite limits.

Clint wondered if the cancer cure Dave had learned about in time to cure a lesion on his forehead would work on what he had. That one worked on prostate cancer, Dave had tried it for the lymphoma and it had worked. He had tried to get it known, but was thwarted by the drug companies who would lose their lucrative chemotherapy market.

What was the plant? Ambrosia?

Yes. It also cured leishmaniasis, a scourge second only to malaria. It was almost a weed in places, but no one knew about it and news about it was silenced.

In the name of profits.

Don't get into that shit now. You have to keep yourself away from depression. That's vital!

He went inside for his first cup of coffee, then swam off the deck for awhile.

The rest of the day was on the computer and moving around Bocas Town, talking to old friends, half of whom were glad the touristiest parts were now concentrated at Drago and half of whom cried about the lost money when the tourists didn't stay there.

Same anywhere in the "civilized" world. Liberal and conservative ideas. Clint was glad the terms didn't really apply to comarca life.

The next day was a repeat. He was holding his own with the headaches and found they were slightly less.

The next day started the same, then he got a call. Faith Richards. She said she and a man from the states, a man called John, were flying into Panamá in about four hours. John had always wanted to see the pirate ship at Soloy (book 51: *Dead Man Talking*) and she could use a vacation. They might run into him there or in David. They were going to make a week or more out of the trip.

So! She came through! He was actually going to go onto the comarca! He was going to try to find a way to steal the artifacts in the museum. That was the thing no master criminal had been able to do. In fact, four had been caught and had been executed. Comarca law demanded that anyone caught taking anything from the museum was to be executed. Period. No mitigating circumstances. No technicalities. They were stealing from the comarca. Anyone caught stealing from the comarca was to be executed. Next case!

Could he get the rest of the bunch onto the comarca? Comarca law could end this scheme in a very final manner.

No. Horvath was keeping his name out of it.

There had to be a way to connect them. It would then be a matter of conspiracy all the way.

Faith would bring Horvath to the comarca. She wouldn't do more. It was up to Clint to figure what he would do and counter it. That was part of the game to her.

Could he do that?

He simply didn't know enough about Horvath. He would have to go on psychology.

He had easy access to drugs. He could try to drug someone. He thought he was clever. He would be the type to ... he financed those movies. He might try some of that phony technological crap. They depended on a place being closed for the master criminal to be able to use the gadgets.

The museum never closed.

What would be his options?

Clint called Silvio, who was the general manager of the pirate ship museum. Every six hours the separate sections were closed for half an hour for the cleaning crew.

"Well, Mr. Horvath! Surprise, surprise!"

Clint called Penceros and said he was going to be in Soloy for a day or two. He would then go back to Bocas Town. It might be unwise for him to be in Bocas Town when Clint got back. Penceros said he had no intention of ever going to David or Bocas again.

Clint smirked and called for his special helicopter pilot he hadn't used in more than three years to pick him up and take him to Soloy. Luckily the chopper was free for a few hours.

"Let's get this boat in the water – or the chopper in the air – or something as trite!"

Clint went directly to the museum, where he was greeted warmly by many of his friends. Silvio was getting old now, but was still a powerful man. He had a very sharp mind and a wonderful sense of humor.

Clint explained that this man was behind a plot to steal Ngobe land. The silver was important to it in that it was used to set a precedent in the courts that would haunt the Ngobe until they had nothing left unless it was stopped now. It was also something to educate the Ngobe about the methods that would be tried in the future, when there was no Clint Faraday to discover the plots.

"What this man will do is try to steal things from the museum. He feels he is smarter than a bunch of savages, but he also knows the risks he'll be taking. He knows he faces success or death.

"Silvio, he doesn't feel. If he loses he will say, 'That's the way it goes!' He may have a slight fear that his execution will be painful, but that is all."

"We do not torture, even in a psychological sense, unless a dire situation arises where it is necessary. That is for the socalled civilized world. He will be executed, not held for years with a little hope, then a ceremony where he is strapped to a table or into a chair with time to fear and hope there will be a reprieve, which is an extension of the torture, no more.

"We will not have a crew of very expensive lawyers getting rich and preachers and social workers keeping the family in a state of mental torture or newsprint and television milking it for those years.

"He will be tried, convicted and executed in a matter of a few hours if the evidence is there. Next case. That has been made clear to the entire world."

"Exactly what I planned."

"You set him up? We will have to consider that, Clint! You know that! It would be using the Ngobe, though it would be to our advantage to stop this."

"No, Silvio. I think you know me better than that. It was suggested by another, a person very much like him. All I've done is point out that no one has ever been smart enough to steal from the museum. The four who tried are dead. Executed.

"Another person even suggested that. He knows the risks exactly. It is how he thinks. He's totally empty of emotions. He has made himself into a billionaire, meanwhile learning money and power are empty, yet he continues. It's a basic death wish. We'll be the vehicle that delivers his wishes. He knows that one day he'll fail.

"Silvio, he has no emotions, no feelings. It will be like turning off a misprogrammed computer."

"Yes. I have met the type. He will figure he screwed that one up. Sad. Pass the yuca, please."

They decided to let Horvath make the plan, they would observe, it would end – if he was stupid enough to actually try to steal from the museum.

"It will be something small, just to prove he was smart enough to do it," Silvio suggested.

Clint shook his head. "It will be physically small, but something that will be noticed soon. He can't gloat if no one knows about it."

"We will see what he plans and how clever he actually is. He cannot buy his way out of it here. We have more than ninety billion dollars in the bank for the people. I think he cannot bribe anyone here!"

"He'll try to do it himself. Buying his way out of it might come later, but he'll have failed by then."

Silvio nodded and sighed.

Clint watched as the private jet landed in David. Faith and Horvath got off and went to the Ciudad de David, where they booked the penthouse. Clint kept them in view.

His cellular buzzed and he answered.

"Hi, Clint! Faith Richards here! I came to David with a friend who wants to see more of Panamá. He's been here before, but wants to see the pirate ship at Soloy. Pictures don't show much.

"Could you arrange anything so he doesn't have to do the tour bit?"

"No. I don't have any pull there. He doesn't have to go along with the tour. He can go as an independent student of history and wander around all he wants. I can probably arrange a special price or that he not be restricted to the time he spends there."

"It's a hundred dollars an hour. He's paid for ten hours and can go tomorrow. I'll go for maybe an hour. I'd like to see it.

"Are you in David?"

"Close."

"Dinner tonight? You know the best places. I'll introduce you to John."

"You went to the better places when you were here. I don't get into David much anymore. I'm not up to date."

"What was the name of that open air place with the great shrimp and sizzlers? Typical or something?"

"La Tipica?"

"I liked their food and it was a nice enough place. I don't like the overdone fancy snobbery places.

"There? Seven?"

"Okay. Sounds good to me."

"We'll catch up then! John wants to wander around town a little. I'll shop. See you tonight!"

They rang off. Clint went to the Alcalá for a room.

Maybe tonight he would learn what Horvath planned, though it wouldn't be necessary. He wasn't going to be out of sight for a second. There were a lot of Indios in David. It wouldn't be necessary to have just one or two followers for Horvath to spot.

They had as many as needed. Horvath wasn't going to see the same one too often.

"Clint! I almost didn't recognize you! I thought you were in your eighties. You look like your sixties."

"Hi. Faith. I'm ninety in two months. You're as stunning as you were. Glad to see you don't play the bimbo game anymore."

"A bimbo running two corporations doesn't play, and I'm as much older as any of us.

"This is John Horvath. Clint Faraday."

"The famous detective. I've heard a lot about you, mainly from Faith." Horvath said.

"I remember reading something about you. Head of a very successful corporation or something. I don't keep up with that stuff. I live on the comarca and live like the natives, for the most part."

Faith laughed. "Clint has a few million in the bank and works like the Indios. He digs yuca and cuts timber and all that."

"I'm Ngobe. I live like my people."

"Yes. You were declared Ngobe. I heard about that," Horvath replied. "I'm far too spoiled to ever want to do physical labor.

"I don't know, though. You're ninety? You could pass for sixty five easily. People like me look ninety when they're sixty five, not vice versa."

"It's good genes and keeping fit." They chatted, had a delicious meal, then went to Peter's bar. Horvath said he was going to Soloy the following day to study some at the pirate ship museum. Could he get a flight or would he have to take a bus?

"You flew in, Faith said. Didn't they tell you the landing strip at Soloy is better than Malek?"

"I flew in my own plane. I didn't know I could go there directly!"

"Yeah. A flight there and back, twice a day. Lots of Europeans and a lot of North Americans fly there directly," Clint explained. "You have to get reservations for the field. It's full a lot of the time. I can call Silvio, the director, and see if they have space.

"What kind of aircraft?"

"Lear executive twelve."

Clint took out his cellular and called Silvio. A plane was leaving later tonight. The next one due wasn't reserved specifically for tomorrow. Horvath could come. Clint handed him the phone.

"How much are the fees. I'll bring the cash," Horvath said quickly.

"Fees? Oh, let me see. Medium-sized jet. Eighty five dollars and fifty cents per day."

"We prefer credit cards to cash. It's easier."

"I'll be there at what time?"

"Anytime after six thirty AM."

"Six thirty one!"

"No. Make it six thirty seven!" Silvio returned with a laugh. "The commercial inflight, you know. No need wasting fuel circling for six minutes."

The rest of the night was pleasant. Horvath was an excellent host and seemed a very friendly type. Clint could like him if he didn't know it was a facade that was part of the psychology of that group. Horvath, like Faith, was an expert at projecting emotions. In reality, they felt nothing. Being excellent spontaneous actors was a survival trait.

Faith suggested Clint stay with her in her suite.

"Same old me. My wife. Period."

She laughed. "I'm jealous as Hell of the bitch! That's the first turn-down I've gotten in ten years!"

They parted. Clint said he might see them in Soloy. He had to go there. They may still be around.

"You can go with us!" Faith cried.

He said it would probably be more comfortable than the helicopter he rode around in.

"You still ride around Bocas on a motorcycle?" Faith asked.

"No. I don't drive. I think it's not smart to drive a car if you're over eighty five. Definitely not a bike."

"We'll see you at five thirty at Malek," Horvath said. "Get up early and be there or we go without you!"

Clint laughed. Faith said she didn't doubt he was always up before five. He was always having his third or forth coffee by then.

Clint soon went to his room and set the alarm for 4:30. Tomorrow, show time!

The sleek jet made a perfect landing and drew into the open plot where it would stay until they left. Horvath was eager to get directly to the museum. Faith would go for about an hour, then would wander around Soloy. She booked a flight back to David at noon.

Clint went into the museum with them, where the magnificent old pirate ship was sitting on the actual old drydock cart it had rested on for almost a hundred years before it was brought to Soloy. The silver plated cannon was still in its place, as were the other artifacts in their cases. Swords with jeweled handles, gold doubloons, art works, tapestries and normal things used on the old ships.

There were rooms where the records and logs from the ship were displayed and where different kinds of booty from the ship were shown. There were the original videos from when the ship was brought through the canal, the fantastic approach at sunrise with the cloud bank behind and the crew, descendants of the original crew along with Clint and his family and the president and first lady at the time.

Tyna was a spectacular beauty, even among the Ngobe. Horvath said he could see why Clint turned Faith down!

"The problem with the bitch is that she's that good looking and a great person with it! I could stand her if she was like normal people and acted like she pissed champagne and shit ice cream!" Faith complained. "You can't help liking her.

"I heard from several people that your daughter is almost as beautiful and your son is the sex king of the comarca."

Clint laughed. "He's more like me. He *was* the sex king until he got married. Nicole is a truly beautiful woman."

"Is it true your son was raped when he was eight years old?" Faith asked innocently.

"Raped? No. He wanted to see what it was like and was with a good friend who was about fourteen and tried it," Clint replied. "He said it was okay, but not special. The Indios don't look at those things like others."

"Your son tried homosexual relations because he wanted to see what it was like and told you about it?!" Horvath cried. "I'd think you'd go ballistic!"

"It's part of life. We Ngobe don't try to pretend life is any different than it is. From about thirteen to sixteen or so kids want to experiment. The only difference is that we don't sneak around and lie about it. It doesn't do any damage to them when it's not put on them as a guilt trip. He wanted to know. He found out. He ran around with his special group like kids and teenagers will. I don't doubt for a single second that he tried a lot of things from both ends. I don't doubt that he had special relationships. Big deal!"

"You had a rather wide open life, I guess. I wasn't raised that way," Horvath said.

"To tell the truth, I didn't. I've never had any direct homosexual encounters, though a couple of times I think I would have, even after I became Ngobe.

"If anything had happened to me in the states, I would probably react a lot differently than I do. I would have all kinds of guilt for things I didn't control and would be a different person than I am.

"What I actually felt when Nito told me about it is a lot different than how I acted. I wanted to kill the bastard who screwed my son, but I just asked if he liked it. He said it wasn't special, but he didn't *dis*like it.

"I know it's just life. It's the way it is, not how you want it to be. Fight it and you're miserable. Accept it and it doesn't bother you. All it says is that Nito is a normal kid who tries things normal kids try and doesn't feel guilty or try to hide that he's normal.

"If he'd been raped, there would be a dead rapist and he wouldn't be any different than he is. He would know it wasn't his fault and he would be stupid to feel guilty about something he had no control over.

"I would kill the rapist. I would have an 'Oh, really? That was wrong. No one has a right to do anything to you that you don't want, but that's life!' He would never know how I felt or how I reacted.

"What the Hell brought this on?"

Faith laughed. "I was pissed that you turned me down and wanted to get in a dig. It backfired, but I had to expect that with you. Back home, telling a man you knew his son had gay relations would make the guy go, as John said, ballistic.

"No more! Let's look around this place. It's fantastic, really."

A man came from the offices with a mop, broom, bucket and rags. He hung a sign on the door of the records room that said it was closed for one half hour for maintenance.

"I thought the museum never closed!" Horvath said.

"A room at the time. They have to clean them. Each room is closed for a half hour a day, except the main room with the ship. That's closed in small sections that don't interfere with the tours," Clint replied.

"Oh! There's the one I want to see! I'm a woman and all that jewelry is a big draw!" She pointed to the historic artifacts door.

They went inside, where there were some hundreds of closed cases with emeralds, rubies, diamonds, opals, sapphires, and others displayed. The first case inside the door had a huge emerald in a solid gold setting with twenty diamonds around it. It's estimated value for the jewels was twelve million nine hundred thousand dollars. It's historical value wasn't possible to appraise.

Clint said he had to get to a meeting, so would leave them to their own devices. He left.

Faith looked around for almost two hours, took a lot of pictures, and left. Horvath stayed for five hours and would come back the next day for the other five.

Clint didn't see them the rest of the day. He observed Horvath through the system in the museum. Horvath would be surprised at the complete covering of every inch. Everything was recorded.

"Ah! Here he comes now!" Silvio said. He and Clint and the four regular operators of the surveillance system were in the security section office. "You say he will try to take something from the jewelry room. It is the fourth cleaned, so he will try then. We will see."

Horvath wandered around until ten minutes before the room would be closed for cleaning. He went into the room and studied it carefully. When the man announced the room would be closed for half an hour everyone else left. He slipped behind a case, then under it when the man checked. The man went out. Horvath went to a case that held six major artifacts with emeralds as the centerpieces. He took something from his briefcase and quickly opened the lock, took a piece out, and relocked the case.

He went toward the door just as it opened and the cleaning man came in. He slipped behind a case and waited. The man went past. He slipped toward the door. The cleaning man turned and saw him. He moved close and said something. The man said "No," and shook his head.

Horvath suddenly swung a hypodermic syringe at the cleaning man, who collapsed almost immediately. Horvath headed to the door and opened it – to find Clint, Silvio, and two guards there.

Silvio went to the cleaning man and checked his pulse. He shook his head.

"What was it?" Clint asked.

"Curare."

Clint shot him exactly between the eyes.

"Judge finds him guilty of murder and of theft from the museum. Execution is ordered," Silvio said sadly. "Clint, I never believed for a second he would kill anyone. I never did!"

"I didn't either. He's named as a conspirator, but that isn't proven to any extent."

"It is on the comarca. Get them here and we end this scheme in a permanent way. This was too much, too far."

Clint nodded. A crew came to take Horvath's body away. Another crew came to take the cleaning man's body out and to return the necklace to the case.

"It would seem our schemers are now one down," Silvio said sadly.

"We have to end this!" Clint snarled. "We can't touch them without the ... clear evidence. All I have is supposition.

"I don't have time! Damn it, I don't have time!"

"You'll think of a way. You always do. Conspiracy to fraud won't be much, but it will allow us to protect ourselves in the future. We take what we can get. This Horvath was the backing, so it will have to wait for them to get other financing. Perhaps, with it then shown it was a conspiracy to defraud, they will not find other financial help."

Clint shook his head and said, bitterly, "It's not enough. All I really have is the threats with supposition about the rest of it.

"I'll have to think on it."

Faith Richards came into the office. "I hear Dear John isn't a problem anymore."

"Faith, he killed a man," Clint said. "We never figured he'd do that. It went a lot further than I ever anticipated. I'll feel guilty about that."

"I never figured that, either. I thought he'd simply say he tried. No go. Didn't feel a thing. Shit!

"I'm sorry about your friend. You said you would blow his brains all over the sidewalk. You wouldn't have done that if he didn't kill that man, would you?"

 Clint thought. "Probably not."

"I'll go back home. This is really an interesting place.

"Should I arrange for someone to come after his jet?"

"No," Silvio said. "He committed a murder on the comarca. Anything he had on the comarca is now comarca property and will be given to Edwardo's family."

"That seems fair enough," she replied. "I think I like the law here. No bullshit. Here's what the law says. That's the end of it. Go bribe somebody else someplace else."

"Uh-huh."

Clint sat at his computer in Bocas Town to bring up all the things he had. It was complete, to his mind, but a court wouldn't consider it except for the threats, which were videotaped and conclusive. Making the threats would get him a restraining order, no more. Unless they were acted on. If they were acted on, it would authenticate most of whatever else he had. Maybe.

This had to end. He wasn't thinking nearly as well as before and knew it. He simply would not and could not let his people down.

He spent some time considering what he had. He added about Horvath being the backing and how he had been executed on the comarca for killing a man and stealing from the comarca.

If he brought them up for the threats, would that stop the financing enough? Would it result in not going ahead with the scheme to set a precedent?

No way. He had to have much more serious charges against them.

He sighed and went to the surveillance computer. It would help his case, minimally, that Flores and Forbes were in his house searching for something. It could be surmised that something was what it actually really was. Evidence against them.

If he caught them in his house after those threats he could defend himself in whatever way seemed advisable. Like a shot between the eyes.

That would get Forbes and Flores out of it, but they weren't the main objective. He probably couldn't tie the whole conspiracy to that. They had it set up to make it look like Forbes and Flores were acting on their own. They would have to do something to make the court have to act on the evidence he supplied. Something a clever lawyer and crooked court system couldn't get around.

He knew one way that would work. One way they would have to use the evidence he'd gathered.

He sighed again and took another pill. The headaches were reduced to a dull background feeling that wasn't really pain, but that wasn't really not pain.

He didn't have long.

He sat at the computer to explain what the doctors found and what he felt. He finished with, "Tyna, I love you more than it is possible to relate. You too, Nito and Nicole. You have all proven to be the kind of people who give me constant pride. If there is an eternity, you will not be forgotten for one second in that time.

"Judi, you have been my truest and best friend since I met you. At times, you were my rock.

"My people, you have given me a life that is full and pleasant. You have given me a philosophy to not fight nature, but to join with it.

"Sergio, Silvio – all my friends on and off the policia, I love you with a never-ending pride of having you in my life.

"I am not going to be around long. I do not want you to grieve for me. I want you to know joy in that I was inspired by you all, that you gave me a wonderful life that leaves me without regrets. I am not a good man, and not a bad man. I am me.

"Nick and Janet and CD and Alma, you have become very special friends who I know will help my people and my family at anytime you are needed.

"I will finish this later. My pain pills are making me groggy and confused. I just want this recorded for when I can no longer say what must be said.

"Nito, protect the comarca and our people. I know you will."

He turned the audio off, but left the video running.

He went into Bocas Town and to the Reef, where Naldo said Flores and Forbes were meeting. He went over to their table to say their financing seemed to be in jeopardy.

"So. You set a man up so you can shoot him. Maybe he wasn't our only source," Forbes snarled. "You'd better watch your back, Faraday. What goes around comes around."

"Ah! I see you got the point! I'll get the records I need in the next day or two and your little scheme will end – *then* you get sent back to the states and will *not* come back to Panamá again!"

"Er, records?" Rancheros asked.

"You can't hide from your past with anyone who knows how to find things comes into it. It's what I do. I've got some things you thought were buried. Guess what! They've been dug up.

"When I add them to what I already have, you're gone. All of you.

"Enjoy your meal. I hear prison food here doesn't quite make the five star gourmet standards you wish to become accustomed to." He turned and walked away.

Now to see if they would do what he felt they would.

He went back to the house to set up a little device on his deck. He straightened some things and washed all the dirty dishes.

He sat to make a short recording, then called Judi, who was, as he knew, in Changuinola. He asked her to bring some of the sour cream they had in Romero's there. He couldn't get it in Bocas or Almirante.

There was a call from in front. He switched on the surveillance system and said to come on in. He was at the computer.

Forbes and Flores came in with, as he had hoped, Rancheros in tow.

They argued about a few things. He baited Forbes into following his nature and making some threats, including him getting a bullet through the head like he had done to Horvath.

He ordered them out of his house.

He then went to the deck to sit at the little table there with a cup of coffee. He switched on the recorder at the place where he left off.

He positioned himself exactly and pushed a piece of coat hanger wire he had been making holding clips for the orchids from onto a hook affair on the railing on the deck over the water.

"... death by murder of well known detective, Clinton Faraday, Ngobe by declaration.

"Detective Faraday was working on a case where a fraudulent scheme to steal Indigeno property on the comarca Ngobe Bugle was exposed. The principles of the case were in his home, where his secret security system recorded an argument in which one of those people threatened to shoot him between the eyes. It seems the threat was carried out. Clint, as his friends called him, was shot between the eyes only moments later.

"The security video/audio recorder showed that one of those people came back and shot Clint, then threw the pistol into the sea. Police have recovered the weapon.

"Here is special detective Geraldo Herrera of the Policía Nacionál, who is investigating the case."

"Thank you, Pamela.

"I was trained by Capitan Sergio Valdez, ironically a man who was trained by Clint in investigative methods. This murder had saddened police in Panamá as well as most Panamanians. He will be missed."

"Can you tell us of anything not restricted by the investigation?"

"Yes. Clint left instructions from some time ago that, in the event of his demise, all investigation is to be available to the police and public. He believed strongly in the transparency laws.

"Clint left quite some collection of papers and videos concerning these people, proving they were in a conspiracy to defraud the government and the Ngobe people of their land. One of those videos was of Clint's last moments.

"It does not show the actual shooting. The perpetrator was between Clint and the camera, but it shows more than we need. That is because it is a conspiracy, so it matters not who physically pulled the trigger. Legally, they each and all pulled it.

"We have the original and have studied it closely. We can know it was not in any way tampered with. If the perpetrators had known of it, they would have destroyed it, not tampered with it.

"Because it cannot be modified, we can show it on television. It does not show the actual murder."

A scene of Clint sitting at the table reading a paper came on the TV. There was an indistinct sound from a distance. Clint called that he was on the deck. Come on in.

"The cameras are both sound and radar directed. They follow the motion, so will move from one to the other," Herrera said.

A man wrapped in towels so only small details could be seen came in and went to move between Clint and the camera.

"Well. So you came back. I've said all I have to say to you," Clint said sharply. "Why the disguise? It could only be one of you three, and the shoes tell me which one."

There was a shot. The form threw the pistol out into the bay and went back to the house and out of sight. Then there was only the picture of Clint slumped over the table.

"The shoes never showed enough for us to identify, but we don't need it. That statement tells us it was definitely one of those conspirators, so they are all equally convicted of murder preplanned."

"What do they say about it? The, uh, conspirators?"

"Exactly what could be expected. That they were together at all times and that no one went back to Clint's house. As it is a clear conspiracy as shown by the carefully researched information Clint left, they have no credible alibi. Certainly not with that video!"

"I understand there was another person in the conspiracy. A Sr. Penceros?"

"Yes. He was not, according to Clint's investigation, part of it by his own choice. He is and was at that moment in Panamá City. As he was unwillingly in the group, had actually helped Clint in his investigation, he will not be charged unless further negative information against him is brought to our attention.

"To the Ngobe Nation and to Clint's family, we wish to say that the Policía Nationál are in deep grief over this terribly shocking loss to law enforcement, and more because Clint was as much as a personal friend of every honest police officer here and elsewhere."

"We thank you, Capitan Herrera. We in the news also grieve for a lost friend."

"CD, can we talk in private?" Nick Storie said.

"Yes. I think you saw what I saw."

"What's wrong!?" Judi cried.

"Nothing," CD Grimes replied. "This is what Clint worked for. That conspiracy is ended and will be a lesson to anyone else who tries such a scheme. It's about a piece of evidence the police seem to have missed. It doesn't really affect anything here. He's saved the comarca again."

CD and Nick went down to the dock at their place on the island.

"Well, Nick? Was it the hand pushing the surveillance system switch or the rod?"

"Both. Should we point it out to the police?"

"No. It was the only way. I saw the medical report. He had a tumor that would have surely killed him before he could get the legal stuff together.

"So. He made that recording to that moment and switched it on as he shot himself. I think that rod has a lot to do with it."

"It was in a rod holder and the tip was pulled back, then the gun was in some kind of setup where it would shoot him, then be flung out into the bay. He rigged that somehow."

"Note the clip stringer hanging just under where the gun would have to be. I want to know how the gun was held into place and with what? Why wasn't it there?"

"Because it went out with the pistol. It wasn't something that looked like ... those coconut husks! He wedged the pistol into the coconut husk and pointed it where he wanted it. The stringer was tied with a piece of nylon. The nylon had a piece above the knot, just hanging. It was attached to the trigger. Use something to prod the stringer, it pulls the trigger, the recoil yanks a stay off the rod, which snaps into the coconut husk upward. The pistol goes flying out into the bay, the husk drops off the rail and everything's normal. A rod and reel in a holder and a stringer tied to the rail."

Mathilde, the local psychic/medicine woman, came around in her cayuca and tied to the dock.

"It was the only way. Let it lay." She walked up toward the house.

"I guess we have our orders!" CD said. Nick nodded.

Tyna handed Mathilde the guanabana chicha and sat.

"Clint communicated with me," Mathilde said. "He wants you to know he is waiting for you. He does not want you to grieve.

"Tyna, he was in great pain, more than most could tolerate. He had a chance for his death to accomplish something important for us, his people.

"It did.

"He would have died of the tumor in just eleven more days. He would have been unconscious for six of those days. The physical pain would never cease. The pills weren't working.

"He says where he is is almost as much a paradise as this place, that he is in no pain and will never again be, except the pain of not having you there yet.

"There is no hurry. He can turn time off there.

"He does not stop loving you. Not for a single moment. Never. You are and were his happiness, you and the children. He has an amazing capacity for love.

"Nick and CD know he ended it himself in the best way he could that would do the most good for his people.

"Tyna, he is blessed by nature and is happy. Do not hurt him by grieving. There is no reason to grieve. It has nothing to do with any god. It has to do with the universe and the way things are.

"His love will never die for his people or his family and friends."

"I have never known another man, and I won't. I understand and won't grieve. I will miss him, every moment. Terribly."

"No. He says it's alright for you to seek another man. For the companionship and sharing. That is a natural thing. He is confident of your love as you were right to be confident of his.

"He says to try out Guillermo. He almost did a time or two, and he's supposed to be the best. You deserve the best."

Tyna laughed. "Now, that is Clint! I can believe you. You are never wrong. You never lie."

"You will live for a long time. Your children and theirs need you. They will always be there for you.

"I must get back to Cusapín."

She stood and went to the dock and to her cayuca. It was a truly beautiful day. Tyna thought of what Clint said about Guillermo and smiled to herself.

She would ask Nito about Guillermo. Where Clint would consider it, but not do it, Nito would. Probably had.

"Yo, Clint! What would you say about a mother asking her son if another man was as good in bed as his reputation?" she asked.

She felt Clint's laugh and smile.

C. D. Moulton's works are available on most major outlets as printed or e-books. CD writes the CD Grimes, PI, mysteries, the Det. Lt. Nick Storie mysteries, the Clint Faraday mysteries, the Flight of the Maita science fiction series, books on orchid culture and many others of many types. Mystery, adventure, intrigue, science fiction, humor, fantasy, paranormal, mild erotica, and factual.

www.ingramcontent.com/pod-product-compliance
Lightning Source LLC
Chambersburg PA
CBHW050332160726
48002CB00001B/290